The moment of truth

Sienna was holding her phone, staring at her *sure* text in its little rectangle, until the screen went black and she had to unlock it again.

"Hit send," Beth whispered. "And you'll be going out with AJ!"

"You do it," Sienna said, thrusting the phone at me.

"Me?"

"It's your birthday," she said.

"So?"

"And that way we're, like, more in it together," she said.

Leave it to Sienna, who is the most awesome, to include me instead of taking the spotlight for herself in this most romantic moment of her life.

I put my hands on top and slowly lowered my thumb toward send. "You sure?" I checked, hovering a millimeter above it.

Sienna's eyes met mine, and she smiled, all calm now. "Sure," she said.

So I hit send, and just like that, Sienna and AJ were going out.

OTHER BOOKS YOU MAY ENJOY

Bad Best Friend	Rachel Vail
Counting by 7s	Holly Goldberg Sloan
The Girls	Amy Goldman Koss
Hope Was Here	Joan Bauer
One for the Murphys	Lynda Mullaly Hunt
Please, Please, Please (The Friendship Ring)	Rachel Vail
Soar	Joan Bauer
Unfriended	Rachel Vail

WELL,

THAT

WAS

AWKWARD

WELL, THAT WAS AWKWARD

rachel vail

PUFFIN BOOKS

PUFFIN BOOKS
An imprint of Penguin Random House LLC, New York

First published in the United States of America by Viking,
an imprint of Penguin Young Readers Group, 2017
Published by Puffin Books, an imprint of Penguin Random House LLC, 2018

Visit us online at penguinrandomhouse.com

LIBRARY OF CONGRESS CATALOGING-IN-PUBLICATION DATA IS AVAILABLE

Puffin Books ISBN 9780147513984

Printed in the United States of America

Book design by Jim Hoover

9 10 8

To Mom and Dad

Thank you for always seeming so unshakeable in your conviction that I am beautiful, wise, and full of panache, even when I am at my most awkward and unsure. Your love is my foundation and my trampoline, the reason I can dare, my courage and my prod. Also thanks for taking me to all the shows and giving me so many books.

Cast of Characters

Gracie Grant—The one you'd want as a best friend. Confident, funny, bright, loving; a genuinely happy person. But there are things she's not so secure about…

Sienna Reyes—Gracie's beautiful best friend. Quieter, smaller, and sportier than Gracie, but equally fierce and caring.

AJ Rojanasopondist—Tall, athletic, sweet, and suddenly really cute.

Emmett Barnaby—Super smart, fun, witty, deeply kind. Has a winning smile and more going on than he's showing.

Riley Valvert—Very pretty and wow does she know it.

Dorin Baker—Talks and laughs so much. Has challenging hair.

1

THAT AWKWARD MOMENT WHEN

You can't just drop a dead sister into the conversation.

If it accidentally comes up that my sister died, everybody freezes, their mouths hanging open and their eyes wide. Then they shift around awkwardly, muttering apologies, and I have to assure them it's okay, it's fine, don't worry!

Well, that's not at all what happened today. But usually that's how it goes: silence, shuffling, sorry, okay.

It came up more when I was younger, before I learned to steer the conversation away at any hint we might be heading in that direction. Sisters, siblings, death? Find the nearest exit, please. In first grade when we were learning graphing, Ms. Murphy told us to stand up when she got to how many siblings we had. Zero? One? Two? Chairs scraped the floor as kids stood up and sat back down, with Ms. Murphy counting. I raised my hand to ask, "What if I have a sister, but she's dead? Is that a zero or a one?" Poor Ms. Murphy wasn't sure either. She said *Um, oh, it's, oh, ah, your choice?* Then she blinked very many times and erased that graph and switched to *How many teeth have you lost?* That night, she called my parents in for a conference to discuss what had happened and to apologize to them. They explained why I had seemed so factual about the situation, so Ms. Murphy wouldn't think I was a scary unfeeling loon, and comforted her. She retired the next year.

My mom says it definitely wasn't because I had traumatized her.

But Mom is like that, very supportive. Always on my side. Never gets mad.

My dad doesn't get mad either, actually. To be fair, he seems generally pretty unemotional about anything that's not the outer planets.

Except when it comes to the subject of Bret. Just the mention of my sister's name makes both Mom and Dad kind of jolty, though they attempt to hide it. Now that I'm almost fourteen, I try not to bring up Bret anymore. You know how if you drop something on the subway tracks, you have to just leave it? You can maybe still see it, your bead necklace or phone or whatever, but too bad; you can't ever get it back. That's kind of what the topic of Bret is like for us at this point.

But today it came up at Monday-out-day lunch, while AJ Rojanasopondist was insisting that his brother Neal must've stolen his permission slip. Which didn't make any sense, obviously. Why would adorable little Neal want to steal AJ's permission slip?

"It's a conspiracy," Emmett explained, in solidarity with his best friend.

"It's true," AJ insisted. "Neal is evil."

Emmett smiled at that. He has the most genuinely happy smile. It takes over his whole face.

Before lunch, Mr. Phillips had snapped his fingers and told AJ, in front of the whole class, that if he didn't get his parents to deliver a signed permission slip by the end of the day, he wouldn't be allowed to go on the trip tomorrow to the concert at the cathedral. So AJ spent the whole lunch period pleading with his mom on Emmett's phone (AJ's phone was dead, as usual) while simultaneously shoving three slices of pizza into his mouth, practically whole.

AJ Eating should be its own channel on YouTube. Everybody would watch it. I'm not kidding; it's seriously that good. The guy barely has to chew.

He and Emmett had taken the other two chairs at the table where Sienna and I were in Famiglia, so it's not like we could politely not listen to AJ trying to convince his mom that little Neal must have stolen the permission slip out of his binder.

"He just wants to mess me up constantly," AJ complained to us after he said *good-bye*, *thanks*, *I love you* to his mom, and handed Emmett's phone back. We all threw out our used plates and napkins. Sienna and I walked out with them into the sunshine of Broadway and stopped in front of the big group of Loud Crowd kids who were stalled there. "Neal may look sweet," AJ continued. "But he is actually a demon child."

Emmett, whose older sister, Daphne, is quiet and studious, said, "Ugh, demon siblings are the worst." Then he looked at me apologetically, realizing.

"Don't you love permission slips?" I asked, to get off the sibling topic.

"I hate them," AJ said. "Permission slips are my enemy."

"Gracie loves *permission slips*?" Riley Valvert asked, rolling her pretty blue eyes toward her Loud Crowd friends about how lame I am. "That's so sad."

"Permission slips are amazing," I said. "Are you kidding?"

Riley looked blankly back at me. She is basically never kidding, so, fair point. Riley is in the Loud Crowd, but despite how beautiful she is, they don't seem to like her very much. If she weren't so nasty, and so pretty, I'd feel sorry for her.

"I love that my parents have to sign a crumpled scrap of paper," I explained. "And then just that little nothing, which I fully could have forged, gives teachers legal cover to ditch school with us to go do some random nonschool thing. How is that not amazing?"

"Good point," Beth chirped.

"Absolutely," Beth's best friend, Michaela, agreed. She was holding hands with David. They've been going out since the end of seventh grade.

"Wait, Gracie—you can forge signatures?" AJ asked me.

"My own parents', sure," I said. "Yours, not so much."

"But maybe you could try—"

"It *is* kind of random," Emmett interrupted. "Permission slips, and off we go?"

"Right?" I seconded. "I want to marry permission slips."

"Ew," Riley said, rolling her eyes again, this time to Michaela, who shrugged.

"So do I," Emmett said. I love Emmett. He is simply the best. He helps everybody out. "We could have a double wedding."

"Perfect," I agreed.

"AJ, you always forget everything," Beth teased, poking him in the ribs.

"Well, my mom said she'd e-mail in a fresh one," AJ said, wiggling away from Beth's tiny tickling fingers. "But if she doesn't manage it, Gracie, maybe you could . . ."

Since AJ kept talking to me, the Loud Crowd was stuck walking back to school with us. Usually it's just me and Sienna, sometimes Emmett, occasionally AJ. Sienna and I don't really hang much with the Loud Crowd. Sienna is quiet and shy, but like the Loud Crowd girls, she is very pretty and also good at sports; I'm neither of those, but I'm easygoing and fun, which is also like them. We're just not involved in the jostling-for-popularity competition, and we don't go to parties or get asked out or stuff like that.

"Oh, sure," Riley said, rolling her eyes yet again. "Like Gracie could forge convincingly."

I heard Sienna groan. Riley is like a rash to her. But

Sienna is nice to everybody, and nobody wants to get into it with Riley.

Riley sighed dramatically. "Well, I know what you mean, AJ, about demon siblings. My sister and I are constantly up for the same parts when we, you know . . ."

"When you what?" Emmett asked. Wise guy. Though I did appreciate it.

"Oh. We're auditioning for commercials downtown."

"Are you?" Emmett asked, all innocent.

"And print media." Riley shook her shiny dark hair off her face, not even mocking herself, just doing it. "Sometimes they want both of us." She and her even prettier older sister are trying to break into commercials and modeling, a fact she manages to mention Every. Single. Day. "But my sister is being such a pill about going on open calls lately. Gracie's lucky she doesn't—"

"Riley!" Sienna snapped at her.

"What?" Riley rolled her bright blue eyes dramatically. Eye-rolling: Riley's one facial expression other than blankly flawless. "She so is. Admit it, Gracie. Ugh. Only child? I wish!"

Emmett turned his back to Riley and said, "So anyway, Gracie . . ."

"It's okay," I told him.

Just ahead of us, Michaela and Beth giggled at something together. Riley sped up so she wouldn't miss out, nudging past Ben to wedge in next to Beth. Hallelujah.

"Let's just get back," Sienna said. "Hey, Gracie, are we

still going to visit the new tortoises Thursday? Your mom said okay?"

"Yeah, definitely."

"Yeah, Sienna's right," Riley said over her shoulder, oblivious to the fact that we'd moved on to the much more enjoyable topic of tortoises. "We better hurry. If we're two seconds late, they act like we killed somebody."

Now Emmett groaned.

"What?" Riley asked. "Oh, because Gracie? You guys act like Gracie is all delicate or something. Have you ever met anybody less delicate?"

"None taken," I said.

Riley shrugged and went back to whispering to her friends.

"Is she *trying* to be nasty or is she actually an incurably terrible person?" Sienna growled, quietly enough so Riley wouldn't hear, as we crossed Broadway at 110th.

"Maybe she just has gas," I whispered back.

"Ha!" Ben said. "Gas!" I guess he heard me. I shrugged at him.

"She just, ugh." Sienna gritted her teeth and watched her sneakers hit the pavement.

All of us got stuck together in the median, while uptown and downtown traffic flew by on either side.

"I don't know why everybody has to be so *careful*," Riley murmured, still on the edge of calm, her graceful hands resting on her narrow hips. "Gracie said herself that it's okay. Right, Gracie?"

Everybody looked at me.

"Oh!" I quickly said. "It's fine! Anyway—"

"See?" Riley interrupted, smiling so pretty. "I mean, it's not like she even knew her sister. *She* didn't kill her. So I don't see why it's such a *thing*."

The light changed. Riley linked her arm through Beth's and whispered something to her as they crossed the street ahead of us.

Sienna touched my arm to hold me back from stepping off the median and into the street, letting some space grow between those people and us. "You okay?"

"Sure!" I smiled. "She's just . . . being Riley. It's fine. Anybody have gum?"

Emmett and Sienna both instantly handed me their packs. "Thanks." I took one from each and shoved both pieces into my mouth as we crossed the street. "Bet I can blow a bubble as big as my face before we get back," I said.

"Bet," Emmett said.

He won, but not by much.

2

IT'S ABOUT TIME

I do love class trips. I wasn't only saying that to distract, unsuccessfully. I love everything about them. Well, almost everything.

Permission slips are just the beginning.

I love lining up in the lobby, and then marching out those doors in our two lines like we're a messed-up first draft of *Madeline.*

Well, our lines weren't straight and we weren't wearing hats. Or even matching outfits. As usual I was in jeans, sneakers, and a T-shirt; Sienna had on little shorts and a hoodie; some of those girls who wear dresses were in those. Okay, so much for *Madeline.* We look completely not alike—

for instance, Sienna is short and just the perfect amount curvy, her light brown skin completely unblotchy, her nose tiny and adorable. Riley, in contrast, is almost my height but like half my weight, with shiny black hair and ocean-blue eyes and not a single curve or percentage point of body fat on her. The other girls are, like, every combination of race and size, from Beth who looks like a fifth grader at most, to Michaela who looks like she's sixteen and ready to go clubbing, to . . . well, me.

Behind us, two women in sunglasses waited for the light to change so they could push their ergonomic strollers across Broadway toward Riverside Park. Three huge guys and one tall ponytailed girl, all in Columbia T-shirts, argued in, I think, Latin, or maybe they were just premed, heading south on Broadway, parting to let the guy who wanders around saying, "Hallelujah, Jesus loves you!" pass between them, his Bible held high.

"Hallelujah Guy," Emmett said, suddenly beside me.

"I love Hallelujah Guy," I said. "Haven't seen him in a while."

"Same," Emmett whispered. "I was getting worried about him."

"Glad he's okay," Sienna said.

"Hallelujah," I added.

Down the block and around the corner from school, a woman with a big nose and long, slightly wild brown hair (like mine, on both counts) sat alone at a table outside the Hungarian Pastry Shop, reading a book and eating a croissant. I almost stopped right there on the sidewalk to stare at her, because it was like seeing my own future.

And it looked okay.

Such a relief.

The woman who looked exactly like I bet I will look in maybe twenty years or thirty was just sitting there with a novel and a snack, smack in the middle of a Tuesday morning. Nobody telling her to hurry. No bells clanging the news that it was time to go to gym now. Nobody making sure she was safe. She just sat there, fully okay, like she owned the morning as much as she owned that paperback.

It put me in the best mood, seeing that woman with the greasy croissant waiting like a comma on top of the pile of tea-stained napkins. It gave me such a jolt of hope about my future.

"You are so psyched," Sienna whispered.

"Fully," I said.

"Same."

"Class trips are the best invention ever, and also did you see that woman—"

"Right?" Sienna agreed. "The best! Screw electricity."

"Who needs antibiotics?" I agreed.

"Oooh, too soon." She had missed a few days for strep last week.

We spotted the albino peacock as we passed the cathedral grounds. "Hey! Look! They mate for life," Sienna said, pointing. She was quoting my little cousin Shane, who told me that peacock fact last weekend, so I told Sienna. We tell each other everything, Sienna and I. We had decided instantly that that was the most romantic peacock fact ever. It made us love the peacocks (and my little cousin Shane) even more than usual.

"Who mates for life?" Emmett asked.

"Peacocks," Sienna and I answered together.

"Really?" Emmett asked.

"Well, with peahens, I guess," I added. "Usually."

"No judgment. Whatever," Sienna agreed. "You be you, peacocks!"

"They do?" AJ asked, next to Emmett. "Is that true? Peacocks mate for life?"

"According to Gracie's eight-year-old cousin," Sienna said. "The genius."

"Who's a genius?" AJ asked. "Gracie or the cousin?"

"Or the peacocks?" Emmett asked.

"All," Sienna said, "but mostly Gracie." She locked her arm through mine.

That made me so happy, I guess I was smiling pretty huge. AJ tilted his head at me, like he was considering me, seeing me fresh.

And that was when the weird thing happened.

My face was instantly hot like a fever. I suddenly had to concentrate on how to breathe. I honestly could not remember how do it. Which is a problem, because, *breathing.* Such a good activity to stay involved in.

I had to figure it out fresh like I was inventing the process: breathe *in*, and *then* out. As a series of actions, instead of doing both at once and choking right there on my own air, halfway up the cathedral steps.

People in comas know how to breathe.

What just happened to me?

AJ and I have been friends since kindergarten, but for the first time it hit me that AJ is weirdly good-looking. It was actually erasing all my skills, how attractive AJ looked, loping up the cathedral steps next to me. Not that I have so many skills, but normally breathing is among them.

"You okay?" Sienna asked.

"Fhytuynfdts," I said.

"Ah," she responded. "Good point."

Plus AJ is on travel team for, I don't know. Every sport? Not that that's a big sales pitch to me, but still. You can't ignore that that is generally considered key, even if not particularly by my parents or me. Also, wow. He is *very* not unpleasant to look at. When did this happen to AJ and why was I not informed?

He was never taller than I was before today, was he?

It occurred to me that I could be having some sort of weird allergy attack. I had never had an allergy attack before, so maybe that was how it felt. Or a seizure. Or, like, it could be a mental breakdown. Or maybe this is how the zombie apocalypse begins. In which case, I should warn somebody.

Breathe in, then out. Left foot, *then* right foot. So many things I had to keep track of, to maintain my own survival.

I would not even make travel breathing team.

"All peacocks mate for life?" Riley asked, turning up beside me suddenly. "Or just the albino ones?"

"Racist," I said.

Sienna laughed and then AJ laughed too, a short chuckle but still. Not a sympathy chuckle, though. Kind of a rumbly chuckle. An approvingly rumbly chuckle.

Oh no. I tripped on a jutting piece of cathedral step. Sienna kept me from face-planting, yanking me up by the elbow. "Seriously, Gracie. You okay?"

Everybody, take turns! Feet: *right, then left.* Hales: *in-, then ex-.*

The inside of the Cathedral of St. John the Divine is cool even in the finally warm springtime of early April, and dark even in bright squinty Tuesday morning daylight. Luckily, because I was damp from sweat.

When nobody is laughing in a rumbly way about a funny thing I just said or considering me with his distractingly cute head tilted slightly to the side, I still run the risk of drowning in my own sweat. So, just imagine the dampness right then.

While our eyes adjusted to the dark, we all had to bump into one another for a while. *Sorry, sorry,* we kept saying, bonking into somebody else. *Oh, sorry, so sorry.*

"Check out the dragons," AJ said, pointing up.

There were dragons hanging from the ceiling of the cathedral, like this was Shun Lee. Shun Lee is a kooky restaurant across from Lincoln Center that I go to sometimes with my grandparents for dim sum brunch before a matinee at the Vivian Beaumont, my favorite theater in the whole city.

There are white papier-mâché dragons and monkeys in Shun Lee. Always. There aren't normally dragons hanging from the cathedral ceiling. It made me crave dim sum.

"You know what I need?" I whispered to Sienna.

"Dim sum?" Emmett responded, right behind me.

"Yasss," I said, spinning around. "How did you . . ."

Emmett pointed up at the dragon overhead.

Mr. Phillips snapped his fingers at us and then explained that the artist, whose name is something, made the dragons, which in fact were actually phoenixes, not dragons, using industrial scrap materials, to signify something.

Some kids wrote down the facts. I did not.

Because, nothing. No excuse. I just didn't.

"I could totally slay those phoenix-dragons," Emmett whispered to us.

"Good to know," I said. "Sit next to me. In case of an attack."

"Okay," Emmett said. Thank goodness for Emmett. My weird dizzy spell was stabilizing. Emmett and I have been buddies forever, since before I can remember. He lives four floors down from me in the same building. I totally love him.

"You brought weapons with you?" AJ asked him.

"I have them at home," Emmett said.

"Still," I defended him. "At least he has them. And we live only, like, a block from here, so . . ."

"What weapons do you have?" Riley asked him, her eyebrows arching.

"All of them," Emmett answered. "They're all Nerf, but . . ."

"That's not even—" Riley started.

"Perfect," I interrupted, slinging my arm around Emmett's shoulders as Sienna laughed. Her laugh sparkled off the ceiling and walls. The cathedral has that churchy sound-effect thing: every noise echoes, and then you yank your head down between your shoulders. It's just like what the tortoise in the funky pet store down past Ninety-Ninth does when people walk too near it.

"Shhh," Mr. Phillips hushed, because the concert was about to begin. We followed him through the center aisle in two unstraight lines to our seats. I took deep breaths to try to calm myself down. Maybe I'm allergic to AJ and his sudden cuteness?

We're not allowed to have phones out, so I couldn't Google the diagnosis.

I am not a fan of jazz music, so what happened next kind of surprised me too.

I had a book when I was little called *Mysterious Thelonious*, by Chris Raschka. That's how my dad always started the book—"*Mysterious Thelonious*, by Chris Raschka"—and I'd open the cover greedily to get to the story. I remember the book said there were no wrong notes on Thelonious Monk's piano. I was fully in love with that idea. I still love it. That book really made me want to like jazz and also to play the piano with no wrong notes, but I have so far failed completely at both ambitions.

The truth is, jazz mostly sounds to me like all wrong notes.

But today one of the acts in the concert was this guy playing the jazz trumpet, just the one guy onstage alone. He'd puff a note up into the air and let it hang there above his head, and then he'd float a different note up to meet it. So it was like he was playing a duet with himself, and then, counting on those two notes to continue hovering together there in the air above us all, he'd let another note, a slightly weird note, a little *off*, waft up there to dance around with those earlier notes.

So it was like he was playing with time just as much as with sounds.

"Trippy," Sienna said when I tried to explain that on our way back to school.

"Wow, Gracie—you're really deep," AJ said, nodding at me. "I never knew that about you before."

"Right?" Sienna said. "I told you. Gracie is seriously deep-dish."

"Yeah," I agreed, in a voice that sounded much squeakier than my usual husky grumble. "I am the deep end of the swimming pool."

"You are," said Emmett quietly.

And then we had to settle down, settle down, and write a recollection of our class trip, using all five senses.

Taste? Seriously? What is there to say about how a concert tasted?

Still, even if I don't like recollections, I do love class trips. Class trips are the bomb. I love class trips so much, I can practically taste them. And they taste like hot chocolate. What? Whatever. The end.

I didn't write about the woman who might've actually been future me reading a novel at Hungarian. I didn't say anything about how AJ looked at me more during this class trip than the whole year so far combined, or about the time-machine trumpeter. Not even the albino peacock. Those aren't the things to write in recollections. You have to fill in the facts you should have written down at the time, like the trumpeter's name was Something and the cathedral was built on Specific Date.

Eyes on your own paper, please, everyone.

But I was in a great mood anyway, because: class trip day. And it was awesome and fun and also AJ said I was really deep. AJ. And he smiled at me . . . four times.

At least four times. Maybe more. Might have been five times.

The good mood lasted all the way until tonight, when I got the text from AJ. Or, well, until right after that.

3

NOTHING ELSE

AJ: Hey Gracie

me: hey

AJ: Is the math test tomorrow?

me: no Friday

AJ: Phew

me: yah srsly

AJ: Well see you tomorrow

me: kk

AJ: That was so funny today what you said

me: which thing?

AJ: ●●●

And then nothing else.

He started to write a response and then I guess changed his mind and deleted it and *nothing.*

Ugh. Cut off my thumbs, because why does anybody let me have thumbs? All they end up doing is texting two words too much. Did I actually text him: **which thing?**

I checked my phone, and yes, indeed, I did.

Why is there no delete key in texting?

Why is there no backspace in time?

Okay. But the thing is? He is actually really into math. Almost as into math as I am. And math tests are always on Fridays. So . . .

No. Come on. It's not like he was just making up an excuse to text me because of, like, liking me, or anything. Obviously there must have been another reason I'm not thinking of. I am clearly having a simple brain fart. *Think, Gracie.*

There are a thousand reasons AJ might have texted me. Like . . .

Math panic! Anybody could have a second of math panic.

Or test panic. We've had so many tests this year that we're all a little brain-fried. He probably was having a panic *of some kind* and tried Emmett and Ben and Harrison and maybe Sienna and nobody knew if the math test was tomorrow or on Friday, so he tried me.

Eh. Not convinced. AJ is not a panicky person. And everybody knows math tests are always on Fridays, so.

Okay, or maybe he just felt like texting me because we're friends. I should just enjoy that. Let that be enough. Because, come on.

It *is* enough.

But just for one second: maybe he was thinking that I was so awesome today and he was noticing that for the first time. It's obviously possible to notice something new about a person you've known forever. Ahem.

Right, so maybe he thought, *Gracie is kind of interesting. She's, like, fun. Maybe I'll text her! But why?* So he came up with the lame and obviously nothing of: **Is the math test tomorrow?**

Okay, that actually makes sense.

Well, more sense than that he was suddenly plowed into stupid by my blinding beauty and wit. Obviously.

Unless . . .

Unless nothing. Have I met me?

No. Nope, nope, nope. Not going there. That's sexist and misogynistic and shallow. Besides, I mean, I actually am awesome. I love me. *I'd* like me. But obviously . . .

And I'm not saying that AJ is shallow or anything. At all.

Just . . . realism.

But that's fine. I am completely fine with that. More than fine. I'm great.

I am. So what if I typed **which thing?** and AJ stopped responding? That's nothing. I'm still good. I don't care. I have so much to love in my life. Boys? Eh. I don't need to love boys, or any boys in particular. I love lots of things. Generally. And specifically! Like, I love, well . . . I love the color yellow. That's something. Also cookies. Post-it notes. I love that a croissant with one bite out of it looks like a comma, which means pause, which is the completely perfect thing for a croissant to mean. Especially a croissant in the midst of being eaten, slowly, on a warm spring Tuesday morning—because it *is* a comma, in another form. A bitten croissant is the pastry equivalent of a comma. I love that!

Who needs boys?

I love tortoises! Whoa, calm down, me.

I love tortoises. My parents say tortoises have diseases so I can't get one. There is a reason against every pet because, I think, they are (understandably) phobic about dealing with death, and all pets die eventually.

I even love my parents, despite that.

And I love how I look. I do. I totally do.

Well, I'm trying.

No, I do. I look awesome. I have cute toes. It's important—I read somewhere on the Internet, so it's definitely true—to pick out a thing about yourself that looks nice and focus on that whenever you start thinking nasty stuff about how you look. My toes are pretty cute.

So, so what about my nose? It's big? Oh, boohoo. Who cares about a nose?

Or my too-tall height, and probably I could lose a few pounds and . . .

Stop. Cute toes. I am beautiful. It doesn't matter who else, if anyone, thinks so. I know I am beautiful.

I am.

Well, maybe. Maybe really not. Whatever. I don't care. Doesn't matter.

Smile time. Otherwise known as dinner.

What I actually am is my parents' sunshine.

4

THE HANDPRINT-SHAPED BRUISE ON MY HEART

My mom sometimes, like tonight but not that often, serves cookies for dessert on the yellow-and-blue plate my sister, Bret, painted with Mom at the paint-on-pottery place that was near where they lived then, outside Boston. Bret made it when she was six, a year before she died. So four years before I was born, because I was born almost exactly three years after she died. She painted her name, *BRET*, with the *R* just a circle on top of two spindly legs, in blue paint on the yellow, next to a handprint. Her handprint. I guess Mom smooshed Bret's little hand onto some blue paint or maybe she just painted Bret's palm with a blue-dipped paintbrush, which I bet would have made Bret giggle (not that I ever heard her giggle except, often, in my imagination), and then flattened her painted hand against the plate. When I was little, I'd measure my hand against Bret's print. I remember mine fit on hers when I was five, though Bret was six when she made it. By the time I turned six, my hand was bigger than the blue handprint, and now my hand is almost as big as the whole plate. Not quite but almost. My massive paw. I have huge hands and feet. Could a boy ever like a girl with such huge, sweaty hands and . . .

Cute toes.

I never made a handprint plate at a paint-on-pottery place.

Maybe Mom was superstitious about that.

Or maybe she just already had one. How many handprint plates does one mom need? Obviously nobody wants a plate with a huge almost-fourteen-year-old's handprint painted on it; that's just gross. It would be weird. So now it's too late anyway.

Mom doesn't put Bret's plate in the dishwasher with the other plates. She washes it carefully by hand and then dries it slowly with a soft towel and then puts it back in its spot in the cabinet above the refrigerator.

I try not to touch the handprint plate because they didn't let me touch it when I was little and I got used to not touching it. I am still a little clumsy. Fine, not a little. If that plate ever broke, Bret's handprint would be gone forever and Mom would, just, I don't even know what.

5

REALLY SHOULD GET THUMB AMPUTATIONS BECAUSE, UGH

RILEY: Hi, Gracie!

me: hi!

RILEY: Quick maybe weird question—who do you like?

me: everybody!

RILEY: Srsly.

me: oh. srsly? nobody. I hate us all.

RILEY: Do you think AJ is cute?

me: yah. sure. fact.

RILEY: And sweet?

me: you like AJ?

RILEY: Dunno. Thinking about it. But yk, maybe Sienna does too, so, awk. ??? Or not? So, do you know if Sienna likes him?

me: well, I flgtjhwe

RILEY: ???

me: sorry. dropped my phone.

RILEY: Do you think he likes me?

me: how would I know?

RILEY: You seem pretty tight w him lately. Right?

me: I guess? do I?

RILEY: I mean, u r basically friends with everybody, boys included. But, like, not in the mix? YK? Like, not tryna get fixed up with anyone yourself. So, yk, like, a neuter.

me: a neuter? yikes.

RILEY: YK, like Switzerland?

me: ah. sure.

RILEY: So—maybe you could ask him for me?

me: ask him out for you?

RILEY: NO!!!! Gak. Gracie. Just, yk, find out . . .

me: if he . . . likes you?

RILEY: BE SUBTLE THO!

RILEY: ???

RILEY: Gracie?

RILEY: Also maybe you could ask Sienna if it's okay?

me: if what's okay?

RILEY: Good point. Maybe don't say anything to Sienna yet?

me: um okay

RILEY: Promise me you won't tell anybody.

me: okay but then how will I find out?

RILEY: I mean don't tell Sienna.

me: oh um okay.

RILEY: Just see if you can find out who AJ likes?

RILEY: If anybody?

RILEY: Maybe don't even mention my name.

RILEY: Any names.

RILEY: Gracie?

me: sorry yeah sure why not sounds good gotta go

RILEY: U r the best.

me: yass that's right me and Switzerland the best evah

6

UNHURTABLE

All day I tried to figure out how to get into a conversation with AJ so I could casually bring up the question of if he likes Riley.

I was starting to consider going to the nurse, because something was obviously deeply wrong with me. And I don't only mean that I was sweating even more than yesterday, but also that it was surprisingly hard to figure out how to form words. I'm normally even better at talking than breathing. Until recently, both have been reliable skills of mine.

When Sienna has strep throat, she can't talk.

Maybe this was what strep throat felt like?

Or stage two of the zombie thing?

Or maybe it was because, when I think about it, I haven't

actually had a conversation *alone* with AJ since, like, second grade, when we had our one playdate at his apartment, during which I accidentally kicked my foot through his window. Which fully wasn't my fault.

It was AJ's idea to play Ninja Samurai Dragon Cookers that day—I'm almost positive. Okay, maybe it was my idea. Who even remembers? AJ loved Ninja Samurai Dragon Cookers too; it wasn't like I forced him or anything. Let's not play the blame game. And sometimes, if a dragon is chasing you, you have to kick it through the window before you can cook it. Obviously.

"Hey, remember Ninja Samurai Dragon Cookers?" I blurted out, there in the cafeteria at the tail end of lunch. *What?* I don't even know what the conversation I was interrupting was, didn't attempt even a lame excuse segue. I just blurted.

"No," Riley said impatiently. "Anyway . . ."

"You weren't here yet," Emmett told Riley, coming to my rescue as usual. "Ninja Samurai Dragon Cookers was the *best*!"

"Right?" I asked. "Anyway, sorry, what were we—"

"Wasn't that the game where we basically just flung ourselves all over the place, trying to do flips and smashing into walls?" Sienna asked, her small mouth full of sandwich.

"Yes!" AJ said. "I totally remember that!"

"Remember that?" I asked. Unnecessarily. He had literally just said, *I totally remember that!* "Great game," I mumbled. Is it possible to literally sweat to death? Would they put that on your death certificate? *Gracie Grant, age almost fourteen, died of an unfortunate sweat attack in her middle school's cafeteria today. . . . Please send donations in her memory to the Deodorant Association of America. . . .*

"That's when we figured out that Gracie was basically a superhero," AJ said, interrupting my internal self-eulogy. "She kicked out my bedroom window!"

"Did I?" I asked innocently, or my best imitation of innocently. My hair was getting damp from underneath. Maybe I actually was cooking up a fever. *He remembered.*

"Yes!" AJ said, and smiled at me. "You totally did! And bounced right up!"

I had to smile back.

Oh. Oh no, no, no.

I am obviously a terrible person. I not only flirt with the guy I'm trying to fix up with a (distant? but still) friend, but I also have to throw myself a tiny secret ceremony of rejoicing when he smiles at me as a result.

"Oh, I kind of do remember that," I managed. "But anyway—"

"She completely shattered the glass, and not a scratch," AJ told Riley, all impressed. "That's what she said, second grade: 'Not a scratch.' I remember that."

"You do?" I asked. "You remember that?" Oh, for goodness' sake. *Stop.*

"Shattered it?" Riley asked skeptically.

"Completely," AJ said.

I did a pretend hair flip, humbly. "Not partially," I said.

"I don't see how she wouldn't have needed stitches," Riley said. "If she really shattered a window." Like I'd purposefully not gotten cut, as a second-grade Ninja Samurai Dragon Cooker, just to mess with my fixing her up with AJ, all these years later.

"It's a conspiracy theory," I said to her.

Emmett laughed.

"Gracie's made of Teflon," Sienna said quietly, meanwhile standing up and pitching her lunch trash into the basket.

"Yeah," AJ agreed. "You're right. She totally is. It's her superpower!"

"Teflon and conspiracy theories," Emmett said, getting up too.

"Absolutely," I said.

"Ask him," Riley hissed at me as we followed them out toward the multipurpose room. We get, like, seven minutes to eat, and then we have to go do gym activities.

"I'm trying," I said. "I'm working toward it."

"Yeah?" she asked. "Could've fooled me."

"Subtlety," I whispered. "It's my other superpower."

"Wait!" Riley yanked me back. Speaking of subtlety.

"What?"

"Maybe ask Emmett instead."

"You like Emmett now?"

"Ew, no."

"Hey," I said. "Emmett is the best. *Ew*?"

"He comes, like, up to my nose."

"You come up to *my* nose," I said.

"So? I'm not tryna be your boyfriend, so what does—"

"Darn," I said. "I thought maybe I had a shot with you."

"What?"

"Kidding. There are so many reasons you can't be my boyfriend. But what does height have to do with it?"

"There's, like . . . It's obvious. You can't go out with a boy shorter than you."

"Or what?" I asked. "You get suspended?"

Riley rolled her pretty eyes. "You just can't."

"So I basically could go out with Ricky Wu or, well, AJ. My only choices."

She groaned. "Literally every time I see Ricky Wu, he offers to show me a magic trick. It's so annoying."

"Some people probably think that's cool."

"Ew! Gracie, I'm serious. Can you just? Just ask Emmett who AJ likes. Okay?"

"So Emmett could only go out with, like, Beth Ng or Dorin Baker?"

"No loitering," Mr. Phillips barked at us, complete with snapping fingers, so we hurried into the multipurpose room, where we had to line up for relay races. No Ninja Samurai Dragon Cookers in eighth grade.

When did we stop just playing? All we do is activities now.

7

TOTALLY NOT WORST IN GYM ACTIVITIES, SO AT LEAST THERE'S THAT

Dorin Baker hurried over to stand in line right next to me. Poor Dorin. She laughs way too much at her own boring stories. She really is sweet and tries so hard to be friends with everybody. The problem is, if I'm nice, she follows after me for the rest of the day, nodding and laughing, agreeing enthusiastically with any random thing I say. And then she launches into long rambling nothing stories about how adorable her little half brother is, and then self-laughs very loud. And I am a terrible person with limited patience.

"How's it going?" I asked her in the gym line though, because, be a person. And also, I have hair that's a lot too. So, #sisterhood.

"I like your . . ." She hesitated. Hadn't thought it through, I guess. "Sneakers."

"Thanks," I said. "Yours are cool too."

"I'm getting new ones today," she said. "Maybe. I might get ones like yours."

"Cool," I said. "We'll be twins."

She laughed. "Okay!"

We shuffled forward. I was next up.

"Do you know how much they cost?" Dorin asked me. "Your sneakers?"

"No," I said. "Sorry."

"Oh," she said. "Okay. Or do you know where you got them?"

Emmett crossed the line, slapping my hand, and I took off like a shot, or as much of a shot as I could manage. A slow-motion shot of something not very fast to begin with. One time in sixth grade I'd heard Riley say to Sienna, "Ba-boom baboom," as I'd run past them in gym. I'd pretended not to hear her. I never said anything about it to anybody because, really, she was right—so what was there to say?

Other than, to my mom, on our way home, that maybe I needed a sports bra.

She took me straight out shopping, without even going home first. She didn't ask why I suddenly needed a sports bra. She just said, "Oh, okay," and we went right to Modell's. I get a pretty big zone of privacy. Sienna is always impressed by that. Sienna's mom always asks, "What happened?" and fully wants to know. My mom just wants me to be home. She likes having me around, she says, so I feel guilty if I sign up for an after-school activity. I don't have to fill her in on all the details of my friends or school or my thoughts. I just have to be there. Alive.

That day at Modell's she bought me two sports bras and one sports cami, even though they weren't on sale or anything. I was so relieved she didn't take me to the Town Shop. Emmett's mom took Daphne to the Town Shop for her first bras. Their mom was born in the Philippines, but she grew up on Eighty-Fourth and Riverside, so she got her first bra at the Town Shop too. It's been there since, like, Colonial times.

They feel you up at the Town Shop. For generations, the first time most girls in Manhattan have gotten to second base, it's with some heavyset older Eastern European woman in the dressing room of the Town Shop. Daphne told me that one night while she was babysitting for me and Emmett, and I never forgot it.

I still have never been to second (or first or up to bat, honestly), but I have a whole new batch of sports bras now, and I wear them every day because otherwise *baboom, baboom*, just walking down the hall. But especially when you're running against AJ, who sprints as if gravity doesn't yank down on him as much as it does other people. I finished behind AJ and slapped Dorin's outstretched hand.

Sienna was on the other team and, having been hand-slapped by AJ, was already heading sleekly back toward us while Dorin ran toward the far wall, arms flailing and lower legs splaying out to the sides. Like four whirligigs combined into the world's most dysfunctional windmill.

"Not looking good for B team," Emmett muttered beside me.

"Don't see how we make it to the world championships this year," I said.

"Breaks my heart," he said.

I smiled. Emmett cares as little as I do if the team we're on in gym wins or loses. We often end up on the same team, somehow, which is nice. We always talk about whether we're likely to make it to the world championships this year in whatever—relay races or rope climbing or the sit-on-scooters floor hockey game I think Awesome Ms. Washington made up. If we win whatever stupid gym thing we're playing that day, Emmett and I are always like, *We're probably heading toward world domination*. If we lose, we're down in the dumps.

Some days I think if Emmett were ever on the other team, gym would be even less fun for me.

"A Team wins!" Awesome Ms. Washington announced. AJ high-fived Sienna.

"There goes my day," Emmett said. "My career in relay racing is shot."

"I'm quitting school and joining a pack of washed-up ex-relay-racers."

"Good call," Emmett said. "There's really no other way to move on."

When I looked over at the A Team, AJ flashed me a happy smile. Wow, he has ridiculously white teeth.

"Do you know if AJ likes anybody?" I whispered to Emmett. "You know, *likes* likes."

Emmett shrugged and shook his head.

"Could you find out?" I whispered as we headed up the stairs.

"Does somebody like him?"

I nodded.

"Who?"

"I can't tell you."

"If you tell me who likes him, I can find out if it's mutual," Emmett said.

I shook my head.

"And there's a better chance he'll say yes or no than come up with a name himself."

"You know I can't."

We trudged up another flight and then another without talking. As we got to the science lab, Emmett stopped short and turned around. I crashed into him and started to laugh, but his face was serious.

"Is it you?" he asked.

"*What?*" Too loud. Ugh.

"Is it?" he asked quietly. "You can tell me."

"You mean, who likes, you know?" How bad is it that I got light-headed anticipating whispering his name? "AJ?"

Emmett just waited. Not smiling.

"No! Me? Obviously not. Why? I don't . . . I . . . Did he, I mean—why? Why would you think I . . ."

Emmett turned back around and went to our lab table.

I caught up with him and dropped my books next to his. "Seriously, Emmett. Come on. Why would you think, or ask, if I—"

"If it were you," he whispered, "who, you know, likes AJ . . . and if by some chance it isn't mutual? I would . . . It would make a difference in how I told you the news. Is all."

"Oh," I said. "Thanks, Emmett. That's nice of you."

"I'm a nice guy," he said, peering into the eyepiece of our microscope at some pond scum.

"The best," I said.

"Sure," he answered without looking up. "That's me. The best ever."

8

NEED A MINUTE

EMMETT: So, yeah, he likes someone.

me: who?

EMMETT: You sure it wasn't you who you were asking for?

me: y

EMMETT: Y like yes or y like why?

me: both

EMMETT: He likes Sienna. Is Sienna the one who likes him?

I turned off my phone. It was honestly pretty close to dying anyway, so. That could be why I had to shut it down. Maybe it shut down itself.

Mercy rule.

Shut it down. Shut it down. Shut it all down. Shut everything down.

Sienna is awesome. I would like Sienna if I were AJ. I like Sienna, and I'm me.

So that's great. He likes my best friend! Yay!

I don't think it's petty and shallow that I need to not tell her yet. For a little while. A few hours. Maybe half an hour. If I keep the information to myself and deal just for a little while, that's not necessarily . . .

Maybe it is. Let's be honest. It's petty and shallow.

I'm petty. I'm shallow.

And why? Why even bother being petty and shallow, really? What did I even think?

Sienna and AJ would make a great couple. They totally should go out. It's so obvious now that I think of it. Think of them together. It's perfect! They are both so sweet and good-looking and sporty and just . . . plain . . . awesome. Not plain. That's not what I mean. What do I mean? Flat-out awesome. Unblemishedly awesome.

Beautifully awesome.

How could AJ not like Sienna? AJ + Sienna. Sienna & AJ.

Sienna is amazing. Adorable and strong, smart and kind. She's never mean or catty or cutting at all, except, okay, occasionally about Riley, who deserves it. But mostly Sienna is just more . . . Like, she sees the beauty in the world. She always notices a new bird's nest in a tree in Riverside Park when we walk down to do her volunteering thing, or how the light hits the building across the street at sunset and turns it pink. I see more beauty when I'm with her, because she points it out.

And speaking of beauty, she is totally pretty without being into that about herself at all. She's not always checking mirrors, like Riley does.

And she's athletic, like AJ. So they have a lot in common. Which is important in a relationship. If they end up having one. Which they fully should!

Plus, she's generous; she's a good person. She does that thing where you pick up trash in Riverside Park practically every time it's posted. She doesn't complain that she could watch multiple episodes of something in those hours, even just joking, but she laughs when somebody else makes that joke every time. Well, me.

Who *wouldn't* like Sienna? That's the real question.

Sienna speaks Spanish fluently. She can do a cartwheel. She has a tiny adorable nose set just right on her pretty face. It scrunches cutely when she smiles. Which she does, at all my jokes, not just the complainy jokes.

When I plan a bake sale to raise money for the tortoises at Turtle Pond in Central Park, she always, always comes through. Bakes big chocolate chip brownies or whatever *and* brings five dollars to buy the stuff I make, which I would fully give her for free but *no*. She gives her five dollars because it helps the causes I care about. Turtles and tortoises. And their health and protection. Or First Book for kids who need books. City Harvest so homeless people can get food, whatever. She doesn't even insist we do the next bake sale for her favorite charity, the Sierra Club. The Sierra Club is her favorite because it supports protecting wildlife and wild places, not just because it looks like Sienna Club, which is what I thought it actually was, for, okay, longer than I am comfortable admitting.

But anyway, that's the kind of friend and person she is.

Everybody likes Sienna. And now AJ *likes* likes Sienna!

Poor Riley is really the issue.

I'll have to break the news to her, which will be like puking into a fan.

I should get that over with, though, maybe even before I tell Sienna the awesome news about her and AJ.

This will be super-romantic and exciting. We will have so much planning and plotting to do about next moves! All that stuff the Loud Crowd does, all that excitement they've been buzzing about all this time while Sienna and I have been busy doing . . . what? Reading? Baking? Picking up trash in Riverside Park? Ugh. Grow up, us! But look, it's happening for us now! It'll be fun for me, too, obviously. Here we go! I won't be left out. I'll be fully in on it all, because I'm her best friend. She always confides in me. I'm so excited! And happy!

But first I am going to not do anything. Maybe look up some sites online about the care and feeding of a pet Russian tortoise, even though I'll never get to have one. Or maybe I will just kick the wall a few more times.

People think I am nice, and a good friend.

No. They are right. That's the truest thing about me. I am a good friend.

I totally am.

Just sometimes I need a fricking minute, is all.

9

ANOTHER REASON, NOT GOOD, BUT

It's not her fault, but the thing is? Sometimes I get annoyed at Bret for being dead.

If she were alive, I could text her anytime I wanted. I could text her right now to ask how to deal. She'd be the only one I would've told that I was thinking maybe AJ liked me. She would say something like, *Oh, that sucks, but you know what? His loss. You're the best one of all.*

And she'd mean it.

Her opinion would matter most to me, so I'd feel better. She'd still be all wispy-pretty like she was when she was a little girl in the pictures in the red photo album next to the couch—but now, at twenty-three, she'd be maybe living down in the Village, doing fabulous things like going to jazz clubs and being an activist working for a cool nonprofit like Sierra Club. And even if Bret had a boyfriend (or girlfriend) who's just as beautiful and awesome as she is, I would still be Bret's number one on her favorites list in her phone.

Because she'd grown up, Mom and Dad wouldn't have sad eyes. They wouldn't be relieved just to have me with them, safe. They'd be relaxed and happy, like Sienna's parents. They wouldn't think constantly about their kid dying like I know they do now.

So that would be nice too.

A smaller reason I wish she were alive: maybe Bret would buy me a tortoise from the weird pet store on Broadway and Ninety-Ninth for my birthday Saturday. They are getting a new shipment of Russian tortoises this Thursday. I really think she would.

Another reason is: I would have her as number one on *my* favorites list in *my* phone, and she might text me in a second, just to say, *So what happened?* And I would text her back with the news, and she'd tell me what to do.

In the alternate reality version of my life where Bret is alive that I think about so often that it feels almost true, Bret takes me out for mani-pedis every month. We don't care about nails. It's just our excuse to hang together. Maybe we don't even do mani-pedis. I just think that's what sisters do, because Riley said yesterday that she and her sister were going to get mani-pedis this afternoon at the nice place near her, down on Seventy-Second, not the cheap place near my apartment, and they go every month.

Maybe Bret and I meet every Wednesday for tea and croissants at Hungarian. Yeah, that's better. More *us*. And weekly. Suck it, Riley, and Riley's even prettier sister, Amelia: every *week*.

Plus, Bret texts me constantly. She tells me her secrets and I tell her mine. We complain to each other about how goofy Dad is, always searching for his glasses and his phone. We have inside jokes about Mom, like how she opens her big brown eyes so wide like a cartoon character when she disagrees, instead of arguing, and says, "Why read last week's newspaper?" when we ask any question about the past. Bret would have been the one I told first when I got my period. Also the first person I told when I got into my first choice for high school, two weeks ago. And that Emmett got in there too, but Sienna didn't. She just missed. She did get into Dalton, which is her first choice of private high school and where her mom went/wanted her to go, so really it was fine. We just won't be together anymore. I didn't apply to any private schools. They cost way too much for my family. It was a weird sorting moment, seeing who was applying to private and who wasn't, this past fall.

Sienna was happy for me, getting into Stuyvesant. Sienna made it completely not weird between us right away, because she's not a jealous or petty person. She said she knew I'd get in there because I'm such a genius (hahahaha) and she promised I'd kill it there, completely, and we'd stay best friends no matter what.

Bret would know what a good friend Sienna is. She'd think we were the coolest kids in eighth grade, Sienna and I. *No contest*, she'd say.

Bret would have thought I was awesome even if I hadn't gotten into Stuyvesant. Not like Mom, like anything I am—as long as it includes *alive*—is fine, perfect, enough. Bret would (since I am the one who is, as always, making this up, I know this is true) think I am specifically awesome, exactly because of the fact that I love tortoises and *can't* do a cartwheel and think about stuff like how similar the words *coma* and *comma* are. And got into Stuy or didn't get into Stuy, and was *liked* liked by AJ, or not. Specifically.

But no. She's dead.

In reality.

Which is bad for many more important reasons than that, if she were alive, she'd help me figure out the text I need to send soon, now, to Riley, and after that the one I need to send to Sienna. But still, I am petty and shallow, and so that is the big selfish reason I am annoyed with my would-be-fabulous but instead-is-dead sister today.

10

SO THAT WENT SUPER WELL

I decided to just wait and tell them in person.

Mom says you should never text or write anything online that you wouldn't be comfortable with the entire world reading, including Grandma, so, yeah. *AJ doesn't like you—he likes Sienna* is not a thing I would want Grandma reading. Or, honestly, Riley.

I told Mom and Dad I had to get to school early to work on a project with Riley Valvert. Not a complete lie, if you squint. Unfortunately, Dad is a morning person. He was down to get an early start, so we went together, even stopped off in the café downstairs in school for a lemon poppy muffin for each of us and a milk for me, coffee for him.

He checked stuff on his phone and I watched the entrance

for friends. Dad doesn't talk much, unless you ask him a direct question or you get him going on the outer planets. Still, #togetherness.

Sometimes Sienna gets dropped off early with her brothers but not today. None of my friends had showed up by the first bell, when we go upstairs. Mostly it was kindergartners and first graders with their parents, plus me and Dad. I kissed him good-bye in the café and went upstairs solo while he gathered his papers to go to his office on the Columbia campus, a few blocks away.

I sat alone up in the eighth-grade hallway until Riley came and dashed over to me, even though her friends were all in the far corner where they always gather before school.

"Hey, so . . ." I started.

She leaned close to me. Our shoulders touched. How does she always smell like powder? "You found out?" she whispered, her skinny fingers balled up tight.

I nodded, sadly, as a hint.

"And? Does he?" she asked. "Tell me what he said. Wait, did you talk to AJ? Or find out from Emmett?"

"From Emmett," I whispered, still frowning so she would please get it without my having to say, *AJ doesn't like you.*

"And?" Riley grabbed my hand. Her fingers are so silky and slim and cold. "Gracie! Tell me! Why didn't you text me right away? Does he?"

I shook my head slowly, like the Tin Woodman of Oz, in need of WD-40.

"No, like, he's not sure if he likes me? Or who he likes?

Or no, like, Emmett doesn't know?" Her pale face was going paler, which made her lips look even pinker. She was turning into Snow White right in front of me. When I get stressed, I do *not* transform into a Disney princess. My hair expands, my skin develops hideous splotches, and I sweat even more than usual. All of which was probably happening right then as we sat there, side by side.

At least we were keeping our average prettiness steady.

Cool, okay, so that's horrible.

"Um," I said. "He . . . just . . ."

"He . . . just *what*? What exactly did Emmett say?"

"I . . . He just . . . I didn't tell him I was asking for *you*," I reassured her.

"Wait, you did? Or you didn't? Gracie, what the—"

"I just asked Emmett to find out who AJ likes—without saying why—and . . ."

"Oh." Riley let go of my hand. "And?"

"And . . ." I shook my head.

"And Emmett said AJ doesn't . . ."

I kept shaking my head. "Sorry."

"It doesn't matter," Riley whispered. "If he doesn't like anybody, then . . ."

We let her unfinished thought hang between us. I was trying to figure out how to correct that idea, praying for an earthquake to knock down the building and save me from having to tell her. No such luck. When no tremors came, I whispered quickly, "Oh, well, speaking of that, it gets worse, because actually he does like somebody. Guess who—"

Riley narrowed her eyes, her mouth, her whole face at me. "Who? You?"

"What? No! Me? Switzerland? The neuter?" And then I laughed, trying to lighten the mood, but unfortunately it sounded more like the hee-haw of a super annoyed donkey. Though, to be fair, did Riley have to make a face like she'd just eaten a pie full of bees at the thought that maybe AJ liked me?

"Then who?"

Before I could answer, Sienna turned the corner into the eighth-grade area.

Riley's eyes flicked up at her then back at me. I micro-shrugged, then micro-nodded, acknowledging the fact.

Sienna smiled all happy as soon as she spotted me. Oblivious, she strolled toward us. Like it was any day. Like it was yesterday, and there wasn't a crisis. Sienna had no idea. And there was no way to warn her. I could feel Riley stiffening beside me.

Watch out, Sienna! I wanted to yell, maybe throw myself in front of her for protection.

Just then Dorin Baker shuffled into the eighth-grade area. She said a loud general *hi* to nobody in particular, which is what made me and Riley look past Sienna to her. Dorin had gotten her hair cut, and it was, well, drastic. Where before it was this huge cascading mass of frizz, now it was chin-length and triangular.

"Ew!" Riley yelled at poor Dorin. "What happened to your *hair*?"

"I, it . . . I got it . . . It got . . . cut?" Dorin sounded unsure about whether this had in fact happened. Her fingers waggled up, up, up and finally tangled themselves into the short hair, near her right ear. Yup, there it was. Cut.

Riley stood up, planting her fists on her narrow hips. Everybody's eyes flicked back and forth between her and Dorin, as if they were playing invisible tennis.

"Ugh," Riley groaned, stalking toward Dorin through the space people cleared for her. We all know one another pretty well by now, and nobody wants to be in Riley's path when she's in this mood. "Everybody thought your hair was disgusting before," Riley said. "But now?" and then she pretended to puke, miming with her fingers toward her open mouth, and gagging.

A bunch of kids started giggling—Michaela and Beth, David, Ben, maybe Harrison, definitely the strivey hangers-on Fern and Fara—which only encouraged Riley to keep going, keep pretend-puking all over the floor near Dorin's feet.

I knew it was me Riley was mad at—or my news anyway. Not Dorin. Not Dorin's hair. Poor Dorin just had bad timing, walking in at exactly the wrong second. She started gulping air. Tears chased each other down past the islands of hot pink on her cheeks while Riley continued to fake-puke and the Loud Crowd continued to giggle.

And then, horribly, Dorin meekly asked Riley, "You don't like it?"

That just reinvigorated Riley's fake-puking performance, much to the amusement of the entire Loud Crowd plus a growing chorus of wannabes, all enthusiastically cracking up and trying to make eye contact with Michaela or Beth, like, *Yeah, we are all laughing; count us in.*

The thing is, you really don't want to get on the wrong side of Riley, or you'll face the wrath of Riley yourself. The smart thing is just to wait it out. She always stops being nasty within a few seconds and goes back to being cluelessly self-involved.

Which is maybe what Dorin was doing. She's a smart girl. Smarter than I am, turns out. Oh well, whatever; I couldn't be smart one second longer. I knew poor Dorin was getting mugged for a reason that had nothing to do with her or her hair but everything to do with me and what I had just told Riley about AJ liking Sienna instead of her.

I had prayed for this earthquake; it was me who'd brought it on.

To be fair, maybe it was the first time Riley had admitted to wanting something and then didn't immediately get it. Maybe that situation felt so weird to her that she really felt like puking. And she'd just found a convenient excuse in poor Dorin's haircut.

Anyway, once I couldn't deny to myself that it was me Riley really wanted to be barfing all over, and why, there wasn't even much of a choice. Unfortunately.

So I said, "Hey, Riley. Quit it."

Her ice-blue eyes latched on to mine, mildly surprised, but dead calm.

"Seriously," I said. "Leave Dorin alone."

Riley's perfect eyebrows went up a millimeter. "What." More of a statement than a question. Or possibly a suggestion: I needed to shut the heck up.

I needed to say something nice, to ease us all over this. Or funny. Funny would be good. Maybe ask Riley if she needed help getting to the nurse. I never mind playing dumb, in service of a joke or for tension-defusing.

Instead I didn't.

"Really, Riley," I said. "What's that whole weird fake-puking thing even supposed to be? A joke? An *audition*?"

Michaela and Beth laughed in a burst at that. *An audition*, I heard other kids whispering. *An audition! Yikes! Called her out! An audition, like Riley always says!* People were giggling, but not me, and not Riley.

"Or do you have gas?" Ben asked, grinning.

A few people gasped.

"No," he said quickly. "That's what Gracie said the other day about Riley—maybe she just has gas!"

Riley didn't acknowledge him or anybody else. Like a fighter pilot or a sniper, she had locked on to her target, and she narrowed her eyes slightly at me.

11

STRANGELY NOTHING

I fully expected Riley to let me have it then, all the crap she thought about me deep down or even just any nasty stuff that she could dredge up in front of everybody. I told myself to clench for it, get ready, at least for goodness' sake to stand up so I could square off with her fairly and not get literally kicked in the face by her fashionable boot with the cute little slanted heel. But I don't know. I was tired.

So I just stayed there on the floor like gum, with everybody now staring at *me.* Awesome.

Riley tightened her mouth into a fake smile. *Here it comes,* I told myself.

She sighed and then shrugged. Broadened her little smile to show her perfect if slightly pointy teeth to the crowd of tense eighth graders all awaiting the fireworks of a Riley takedown, and flounced into math as the bell rang.

"Well," Emmett said to me as I heaved myself off the floor.

"Yeah, seriously," I said. "Don't know how that turned into nothing."

"So far," he said.

"Hey," I called after him. "What do you mean, 'so far'?" But Sienna was yanking my sleeve, holding me back.

"What the heck was *that*?" she asked. "She is really getting beyond—"

"Eh. Just Riley being Riley, I guess," I said. "But, in bigger news . . ."

"Bigger news?"

"Girls?" Mr. Phillips said warningly, snapping toward the classroom door.

We hurried into class as I whispered to Sienna, "Do you like AJ?"

"AJ?"

"Yeah!"

"*Like him* like him?" she asked.

We sat down at our desks, next to each other, and I nodded.

She shrugged, and wrote a big *Y* on her notebook paper.

Y for *why* or *Y* for *yes*? Either way. I raised my eyebrows twice, in response.

Sienna buried her face in her hands and breathed there for a few seconds. I didn't know if she was upset or embarrassed or excited or what. When she lifted her head, she just stared straight ahead like she was so interested in polynomials.

On our way up the stairs to chorus, Sienna whispered, "Does he like me?"

"Yeah," I whispered back. "Emmett told me." I looked behind us to see if Riley was right there, because, ouch. She wasn't. I didn't see her anywhere. "Do you like him?"

"I don't know," Sienna whispered. "I guess?"

"He's super sweet," I said.

"Oh yeah, definitely," she agreed. "I mean, I like him, sure, but . . ."

"But?"

"I don't know. Anyway. Are you still coming over after school today to bake?"

"Yeah," I said. "We can talk about it then!"

"Okay," she said, but she didn't seem that happy about it. "But we can stop off at the pet shop on the way, yeah?"

"Sure!" I said. I know, I know: no pets for me. Still, I could fantasize.

Obviously.

Hey, there's another major skill of mine: imagining what if something that is never, ever going to happen magically *happened*?! Like: me having a pet tortoise and an alive older sister and a boy who likes me. A sad skill, but still, with that plus the sweating and the cute toes, I am obviously on a rocket to fame and fortune. So why would I care one bit about who AJ Rojanasopondist likes? I got bigger fish to . . .

"What's tomorrow's bake sale for?" Sienna was asking me. "Gracie?"

"Oh. Sorry. Um, First Book," I said, once my brain processed her question. She looked back at me blankly. "They provide new books for children in need, remember?"

"Right, sorry," Sienna said. "I'm a little . . . I can't . . ."

"We could split it with Sierra Club if you want."

"Okay," she said. "Or next time. Whatever. My dad said he'd buy enough supplies for a quadruple cupcake recipe today. Red velvet, okay? White frosting?"

"Great. He's gotten really cute, don't you think?"

"My dad?"

"Um, sure? Your dad is very handsome. But I meant AJ."

"Oh." Sienna watched her feet going up the last few steps. "I guess, yeah. I never really . . . I mean, we've been friends since kindergarten, and I just never . . ."

"Yeah."

"Now I feel all weird."

"You do? Like, can't-remember-how-to-breathe funny?"

"Like, how-am-I-gonna-act-normal-at-lunch? funny."

I laughed. If only that were all, for me.

Sienna groaned and then headed toward the soprano section, where Riley was already stationed, her posture perfect, her pretty face calm and composed.

Maybe there are advantages to not being the one in the spotlight, I decided. I stood in the back row of the altos, with my hands in my pockets. So what if I'm not *it*, not the one AJ has a crush on or everybody expects to be beautiful, perfect, even mildly awesome. I don't want the solo! No, thank you. I'm good back here, singing the harmony, thanks!

I'm just the wingman. Not *just.* I am the wingman! Which is great! That's the best part in any show, everybody knows: the best friend. I'm the one you text when you can't figure out the math or you want to watch a zombie-movie marathon or need to find out if somebody likes you. The comic relief. The neuter. The alto. The harmony. The other one.

I could just turn into particles of mist and float away.

12

UGLY

On our way to lunch, Riley pulled me back.

"Can I talk to you a sec?" she asked.

"Sure," I told her, even though we really do get only seven minutes to eat and I spend a lot of the morning looking forward to the eating part of my day. We went into the big main-floor gender-neutral bathroom. She locked the door behind us.

"Are you okay?" she asked.

"Sure."

"I think we should talk."

"Okay. What's up?"

She glanced at herself in the mirror, adjusting her shiny dark hair over her left shoulder. I waited.

"I understand why you were so rude and insensitive this morning," Riley said.

"Me?"

"I know that you sometimes feel jealous of me, you know, because I'm a model, and my popularity, whatever."

"Riley," I said. "I'm really not."

"Don't try to deny it, Gracie. I see how you react when it comes up that I'll be doing commercials. Even how you're always looking at my bag, my boots, my hair, at all of us, you know, my group of friends—and what I want to tell you is: relax. I'm not mad. I'd like to think we are friends too, you and I. Well, friendly."

"Um, okay, yeah, sure."

"And as a friend?" she said, her voice soothing, like she was on a commercial for baby cough medicine. "I want to help you. So I have to tell you—what's really unattractive? Worse than body size or bad facial features? Is how jealous you're acting."

"Wow . . ." I started, but stopped myself. Mom says people say nasty things when they feel embarrassed or insecure; the challenge for an ethical person is to recognize this and not respond. Mom is an ethics professor at Columbia so we've talked about ethics basically since I was born and she expects me to be ethical. I don't want to let her down, but I think she sometimes forgets that I'm not Bret, angelic and impish. I'm Gracie, big and blunt.

I started again. "Riley, I don't—"

She interrupted, "Beauty, or the opposite, comes from the inside."

"I completely agree," I said. "Well! Glad we had this talk."

I reached for the doorknob, opened the door, and walked out, thinking, *She's right that I'm not beautiful on the inside, either. Just like Riley, I'm jealous that AJ likes Sienna instead of me.*

"And nothing is quite as ugly as jealousy," Riley said, following me into the café.

"You're right," I agreed quietly, so not even the kids at the tables near the entrance could hear.

"Except maybe selfishness."

I stopped without turning around. *Selfishness?*

"I know it's not easy for you to hear, Gracie," Riley continued, right behind me. "But it's what everybody thinks about you. You only care about yourself. Nobody else's feelings matter to you."

"Come on, Riley." I wasn't fighting back *exactly because* I was thinking at that literal second about her feelings! "Stop. Let's go eat."

People looked up from their lunches at us. Sienna cocked her head to the side like, *What's up?* I raised one eyebrow at her; she smiled back, in sympathy. Thinking I was just trying to get away from Riley, who was probably humble-bragging about how much of a drag it is that she has to get her picture professionally taken so often. *Auditions.*

"You march around like you deserve special treatment," Riley continued cluelessly as we got nearer to the tables. "Just because your parents lost a child."

"Wait, what?" I stopped again. This time I turned around to face her.

"But the truth is, that happened way before you were even born," Riley whispered. "It's all just stories you've heard, really. I'm sure it was a tragedy to your parents. Though from what I've read on the Internet, well—"

"What you read on the Internet?" I interrupted. She had saved herself momentarily by being so random that I needed some clarification.

"That's not the point."

Yeah, obviously, milkweed. But still: What? "You were just randomly reading on the Internet about how parents feel when their seven-year-old gets run over and dies?"

"This is exactly what I mean, Gracie. You bend every conversation so that it turns into everything being about *you.*"

I was sweating so much by that point that some of it, horrifyingly, was coming out of my eyes. Or possibly I was starting to cry. Which is too weird. I am not a crier. I never cry. And especially not at this. I didn't feel *sad*! Confused, maybe. *I will not cry in front of the entire school,* I vowed, my back to them all except Riley. *No way, especially not because of Riley.*

"But the real tragedy of *your* life," Riley went on whispering, fully composed, one fist on her slender hip, "as opposed to the tragedy of your *parents'* lives, is that because of the death of their first daughter, your parents have raised you as a veal child."

"As a what?" I managed to croak out.

"As if you don't ever have to take anybody else's feelings into consideration."

"*Veal child?* Are you kidding me?"

Which was a stupid question. She is never kidding.

"Girls?" Awesome Ms. Washington prompted us as she passed on her way to the gym. "What's good?"

"Everything." Riley flashed a smile you'd buy a more expensive brand of toothpaste to get.

"Four minutes," Awesome Ms. Washington said over her shoulder. "Better eat."

We couldn't. Riley and I were locked in on each other.

"I'm sorry if that hurts," Riley said quietly. "The truth sometimes hurts—but then it helps. The truth will set you free, is what my father says. And he's CFO of a Fortune 500 company. So he should know. I'm not bragging; I'm just saying."

"Okay."

"And, truthfully, everyone can see you only care about yourself."

"It's . . . But that's not the truth," I said.

"Gracie, you obviously think you're perfect, but nobody else thinks—"

"No! I'm not saying I'm perfect," I said. "At all! I have, like, a million faults. We could spend all day listing them, hahahaha, but I really don't think that's what—" I stopped myself. I didn't need to state the obvious thing that she was hurt about, right? No. Hold it in. "But not caring about other people doesn't even make the top ten bad things about me.

You know that. Come on. If you're gonna insult me? Is that really all you've got? Veal?"

Riley pursed her pretty lips.

"You can do better than that," I said. "If you're trying to insult me, how about, *Hey, Gracie! Your hair is so out of control, you should wash it with Ritalin*?"

A bunch of kids behind me laughed. I guess I was being loud. Okay, then.

"Or, like, *Hey, Gracie! Your nose is so big, if you wore glasses, you'd need glasses to see your glasses on it*?"

Pretty much everybody behind me was cracking up now.

"How about, *You know what's uglier than your face, Gracie? Racism!*?"

I heard a few kids go, "What!" and a few more yell, "Yes!"

"But to say . . ."

She smiled gently, so pretty, so tight. "I think in your heart of hearts, Gracie," she said almost inaudibly, "you know it's the truth. You only care about yourself—you only *think* about yourself. You hate yourself so much and still so desperately need to be the center of attention, you'll stand here insulting yourself in front of the whole school."

I shook my head. "No, I'm not the one who—"

"Think about it," Riley said, touching my arm gently, briefly, as she walked away.

13

THE PACT

Luckily we were all rushed into the gym to run laps around the room, so neither of us could say anything more. I guess we had both said plenty. I kept my head down to avoid anybody's reactions.

I honestly do not enjoy being the center of attention. I wasn't just saying that.

"Subtle," Emmett said, beside me. No teams in running laps.

"Yeah," I agreed, without making eye contact with anyone but my sneakers. "That's the truest thing about me. Subtlety."

Emmett shrugged. "She's pond scum."

"Thanks," I said.

Sienna slowed down to jog with us. “Amazing, right?” Emmett asked her.

“Gracie is the best,” Sienna agreed.

“You guys, stop.” I appreciated the support, but I also disagreed. “Really.”

“You okay?” Sienna asked.

“Always!”

“What was that all about?” Sienna whispered.

“Dorin,” Emmett said. “Right?”

“Yeah,” I said. “Just, you know, Riley being . . . Nothing.”

Awesome Ms. Washington blew her whistle, so we filed out. Riley and I avoided each other in the halls. I kept my eyes on my books.

“That was hilarious,” Michaela whispered to me on our way in to social studies.

I didn’t say anything back.

At the lockers at the end of the day, Beth whispered, “You are so funny, LOL.” She wasn’t actually laughing out loud, though.

Sienna and I walked out of the building together, without stopping to chat with anyone near the café, even though people were murmuring stuff like, “What’s uglier than your face? Racism.” Hard to say whose side they were on, and I so didn’t want to be on a side, never mind *be* one of the sides.

We got in line for Italian ices from the Coco Helado lady outside school, even though we were going to be baking. Not for a while, though, because we were stopping off at the pet store on our way. Plus icies are mostly just ice, right? We watched Riley flounce out of the school building and into the black town car waiting for her at the corner, her nanny and sister already in the backseat.

"Phew," Sienna said.

"Yeah," I said, and breathed out.

"Did Dorin get picked up early?" Emmett asked, rainbow icie in hand.

"Dunno," I said. "Probably. Icies are mostly ice."

"Absolutely," Emmett agreed. "Food coloring and sugar are nothing."

"Yeah," AJ said, loping over to join us. "They basically don't exist."

We all concentrated very much on our icies then.

"See you guys," Emmett said. He has opera after school on Thursdays, so he has to take the 1 train down to Lincoln Center.

When I told Mom in second grade that Emmett sings at the Met, she was like, *Oh, honey, if little Emmett Barnaby sings at the Metropolitan Opera, I will eat my hat.* Which I thought was kind of an alarming if/then. So she called up Emmett's mom like, *Gracie said the funniest thing about Emmett singing in the—No way, really?* Because Emmett's mom was like, *Yeah, he's in the Metropolitan Opera Children's Chorus.* Instead of eating her hat, Mom took me to see him in *Carmen,* and she ate a smoked salmon sandwich at intermission, which at the time sounded equally gross to me. I ate a cookie and fell asleep before the end, but still it was fun to see Emmett in that. He looked tiny up there on that huge stage, like a toddler. He doesn't talk about it much, but I think he likes it. He misses school sometimes for rehearsals, though, which sucks for me because everything's less fun when he's not there.

When I turned from watching him cross Broadway, the line at the Coco Helado lady had disappeared so it was just me and AJ and Sienna left standing together on the sidewalk. In case there hadn't been enough awkwardness for one day.

AJ kicked at a crumbling bit of pavement a couple of times. Just as Sienna was starting to say, "Well . . . " he said, "I forgot I have . . ."

"Go ahead," Sienna said.

"Oh no, it's okay."

They were both blushing and looking hard at the sidewalk, like maybe a heads-up penny would please appear and give them some luck.

Eventually AJ said, "You don't have volleyball?"

"Not today," she mumbled.

"I should . . . I have . . ."

"Sure," Sienna said.

AJ galumphed back into the school building. Usually he runs so gracefully.

"Well, that was horrible," Sienna said.

I had to agree. There was no getting around it.

"Let's go see some Russian tortoises," Sienna suggested.

We tossed the dregs of our icies and didn't talk much on the way down to just past Ninety-Ninth. We don't need to chatter all the time like the Loud Crowd girls. We just enjoyed the walk, and being together, the sun on our heads.

It had been a long cold winter, and the icies had cooled us enough to enjoy the heat.

"You're so funny," Sienna said, around 102nd. "But you don't need to insult yourself so much."

"I don't usually, do I?"

"Yeah," Sienna said. "We both do, I've noticed. We should try to not do that. Boys don't do it. Just girls. And we shouldn't, you know?"

"You're right," I said. "Okay."

"We'll try to catch each other. We don't have to keep saying how bad we are at stuff, as an antidote to being braggy like Riley."

"Good point." I shrugged. "I might suck at that, but . . ."

Sienna laughed. I love making her laugh.

"This is going to take some work."

"We'll practice," Sienna said. "Promise we'll both try?"

"Promise," I said. "No insulting ourselves."

"So, Riley was on your case about standing up for Dorin?" Sienna asked. Before I could answer, she added, "Riley is such a cramp."

"She so is," I agreed. "Just clarifying: we can dump on Riley, just not ourselves?"

"Absolutely," Sienna said.

14

THINGS I CAN'T GET

The pet shop is small and narrow. When you go in, the balding hipster-dad guy at the counter doesn't say anything, but the parrot on its perch says, "Hello! Hello!"

"Hi," we answered.

"Hello!" the parrot said.

"How's it going?" I asked, halfway down the stairs.

"Hello!" it answered.

In the basement, it's hot and humid. I guess so the reptiles will be comfortable, though there are also gerbils and guinea pigs and some parakeets down there. I don't know, maybe all those kinds of animals like swampy weather. The huge tortoise was near the bottom of the stairs, his head under a shelf, like he was trying to hide.

"Don't worry," I told him. "We can't see you, big guy."

"He's afraid of the speed demon here," said a familiar voice. We looked over toward the back corner—Dorin.

"Hey," Sienna and I both said.

"Hi," Dorin said. "Want to see the baby Russian torts? They just arrived this morning."

"Yeah," I said. We went to where she was standing. There were three tiny tortoises in a tank by her side, still as statues.

"Oooo, so cute!" Sienna said. "They're like pebbles!"

But my attention was caught by the slightly bigger tortoise in the tank closer to me, who looked like he wanted to dig his way out of there, and was determined to do it if it took all night and he had to go straight through the glass.

Dorin pointed at that busy tort. "The speed demon, we call that one. She's got a lot of go in her."

I silently apologized to the speed demon for assuming she was male. "What do you mean?" I asked Dorin. "A lot of go?"

"She was in that tank there, see?" Dorin pointed at a tank by our feet that had a scary lizard in it. "See the sliding door? Torts are not supposed to be able to open those. But this smarty-pants tort, she just opened it up and was marching around, totally freaking out Big Guy, as you called him. His name is actually Belvedere, the big guy, by the way."

"Like Belvedere Castle?" I asked.

"Yeah," Dorin said. "How it looms over Turtle Pond in Central Park?"

"Sure. Perfect name. Do you . . . work here?" I asked her.

Can eighth graders in Manhattan have jobs? Is that a thing and I'm just too *veal child* to know?

"My parents own this place," Dorin said. "So, sort of?"

"That's so cool!"

Her nervous fingers flickered up to her hair, and she seemed suddenly awkward again, like she is in school. It wasn't until then that I realized how different she had seemed, in the muggy basement of the weird pet shop. Comfortable. Confident.

Maybe, like a reptile, she needs heat and humidity to thrive.

"Wait," Sienna said. "The little guy scared the huge tortoise? Or is scared *of* him?"

"She scared him! Look! He's hiding from her!" Dorin nodded, the awkwardness gone again in a flash. "You want to see her go? I can take her out if you want. I'm allowed."

"Sure," I said.

Dorin lifted the lamp off the top screen of the doorless tank the speed demon was in, turned the screen perpendicular, and, with expert hands, no hesitation, lifted the tortoise. "You want to hold her sort of as if she were a hamburger," Dorin explained. "Some of them, like the red-eared slider?" She pointed to a tank across the room. "They don't really like being held much, but this one is so sweet and friendly. Aren't you?"

Dorin put her nose right next to the tortoise's nose, and they stared at each other across the millimeter and the species divide.

Then Dorin sat down cross-legged on the painted concrete floor, so Sienna and I did too. She put the tort down in the middle of our circle. The tort charged right toward me. I know tortoises are supposed to be slow, but this one, not even kidding: she was sprinting. She climbed up onto my foot, lifted her Yoda head, and looked me in the eye.

"Hello, you," I said. I rubbed her shell lightly. I don't know if tortoises can even feel that kind of thing, but it seemed like, an animal looking up at you all sweet like that, you should pet it.

"She likes you," Dorin said.

"It's mutual," Sienna said. "Look at them. True love at first sight!"

They laughed, and I smiled. True love. Careful what you wish for, I guess. The tortoise climbed over my foot, belly-flopped onto the hard floor, and started dashing across the room. "Easy come, easy go," I said. "Shortest love story ever."

"She just, you know," Dorin said. "Why are you here?" Hands in her hair again.

"It's Gracie's birthday Saturday, and she loves tortoises, so we're celebrating."

I loved that Sienna didn't mention anything about my party. She knows who's invited and who is not, obviously. She is such a good person.

"I know you sometimes raise money for the New York Turtle Conservancy," Dorin said. "But you have a lot of causes you raise money for, so I didn't know that was a special one to you."

I shrugged.

"You're buying her a tortoise?" Dorin asked Sienna. "That's really generous. They're not cheap, you know. Plus all the stuff you need. I know you're rich, but . . ."

"No," I said. Sienna hates when people notice she's rich or say anything about it. "We're just visiting. I'm not allowed to get one anyway. No pets."

"Wow, really?" Dorin asked. "I'm so sorry. No pets at all? That's horrible. My half brother would literally die if we couldn't have pets."

I smiled at her, hoping she wouldn't realize about the whole sibling-literally-dying issue and we could just fly right past it. "You must have a lot of pets."

Dorin nodded. "Yeah, but anyway, the speed demon you liked, where is she? Wow, she is really an escape artist! Oh!" Dorin skipped across the room to where the speed-demon tortoise was climbing onto the huge tortoise's foot. "She's already on hold. You couldn't have bought her anyway. So don't feel bad. Even a fish?"

"What?"

"You can't even have a fish? We have some bettas, if you want to look. You don't need a filtration system for them, so . . ."

"Can I hold her?" I asked.

Dorin put the speed-demon tortoise in my hands. We

stared at each other as her little dinosaur legs swam in the air. "Things I can't get," I said to the tortoise. "One—you. Two—boys—"

"Gracie," Sienna tried to interrupt.

"Three," I counter-interrupted. "Factoring."

"You totally get factoring," Sienna said. "And any boy would—"

"Four . . ." I said, moving on.

"Gracie," Sienna tried. "Remember? We're not—"

"Upset," Dorin said.

"Huh?" I asked.

"You never get angry. Or sad. Or . . . You're the happiest girl I know."

"Ha!" I put the wriggling tortoise down onto the floor. She climbed up onto my foot and stopped, exhaled like she was a bus parking, and stayed there, resting on my sneaker.

Never sad or angry, huh? Weird what people think. I'm the most see-through person ever, but people kept getting me wrong all day long.

"Thanks for standing up for me today," Dorin whispered toward the tortoise, as if the speed demon had been the one to say the minimal necessary nothing to Riley. "I mean, I know she's your friend, but—"

"She is not," Sienna said. "We're not friends with her at all."

"Oh," Dorin said. "I guess I just think everybody is friends with everybody above a certain popularity level."

"Riley is a nasty, boring girl who thinks she's all that, but she's so not," Sienna said. "Don't take anything she does personally."

"My mom said Riley was probably just jealous of me," Dorin said. "Do you think that's true?"

Awkward. Um. Sienna and I both shrugged.

"I don't think so either," Dorin said. "My mom always says that when girls are mean to me. That they're jealous."

"Grown-ups always say that," I said.

"They think they're being nice, maybe," Sienna said.

"She told me to say that to some girls in my camp last year," Dorin said. "'You're all just jealous of me!' It didn't go well."

"Oh," Sienna said.

"Yikes," I said.

"My mom is really sweet?" Dorin said. "She thinks saying everybody is just jealous of me will make me feel better, but it doesn't. It just makes me feel like she's either lying or stupid. Why would Riley be jealous of me?"

"Well, plenty of reasons," I said. "It's not like Riley gets to hang with all these animals anytime she wants."

Dorin smiled. "That's true."

"But still, yeah," I said. "It's not necessarily about her being *jealous* of you, why Riley was mean."

"She just has the personality of a blister," Sienna said.

"I'm not criticizing your mom," I said. "But, like, are you really supposed to say, *Hey, Riley, you're just jealous of me*? Because, don't do that."

"Okay," Dorin said.

"Yeah," Sienna said. "If Riley says anything else rude, just look at her like, *Eww, what is wrong with you?* And move on with your day."

"Good advice," I said. *Advice I should've taken earlier in the day. Where is that time machine when you need it?*

"Okay," Dorin said again.

"I'm sure your mom just wants you to be okay," I said. "I think maybe parents hate to see us sad or hurt so much, they're like, *No!* if for a second we feel not okay."

"Does that happen to you, too?" Dorin asked, her pale eyes wide.

"My parents say, 'It's not the end of the world,'" Sienna said.

"Mine just need me to be happy," I said. "All the time."

"Yeah, I definitely didn't think my hair looked as good as my mom said it did," Dorin said, fingers working in the mess of short hair. "But that was a horrible way to start the day, and it felt like everybody agreed with Riley's opinion until you—"

"It looks great," Sienna said. "Makes your neck look long and pretty."

Dorin turned bright red.

"It does," I agreed.

"I just . . ." Dorin said. "You know, my uncle."

Sienna and I looked at each other. We don't know Dorin's uncle.

"He died," Dorin said.

"Oh," I said.

"Sorry to hear that," Sienna said.

"Yeah," I agreed. "Sorry to hear that."

"Five years ago," Dorin said.

"Oh," Sienna and I both said. Even the tortoise on my foot sighed.

"But I was thinking about him a lot lately, and wishing, well, like everybody, that I could think up a cure for cancer, because wouldn't that be so amazing? And I guess, selfishly, like, *Hahaha, all you people who aren't so nice to me? I just thought up the cure for cancer! Boom! What do you think of me now?!*"

"Sure." I knelt down to look at the tortoise because it was too awkward to make eye contact with Dorin and I wasn't sure what else to say and there was a slight risk I could burst out laughing if I looked at Sienna, which you cannot do while in the midst of a cancer or bullying conversation.

"So what I thought," Dorin continued, "was, well, maybe my brain can't think up the cure for cancer right now, but I do have all this hair. I could get some chopped off and donate it, for cancer-people wigs. So I did. Not to Locks of Love—the other one? But instead of people being like, *Oh, cool* . . . I mean, not that that's the only reason why I did it. I honestly wanted to be generous, but you know. But instead I made such a mess of myself, people barf at the sight of me. And when I get upset, I actually puke—it's like an allergy? Like, my half brother is allergic to peanuts, except not like that exactly, because he could actually die from a single peanut and he has had to go to the hospital just from peanut dust and get a shot and it's terrifying because he swells completely up? Like an Oompa Loompa except dangerous and nonfictional? But I just puke. That's it; I'm done. From anxiety. So I ended up getting sent home for throwing up in the nurse's office, where I just went to cry about Riley fake-puking at me. Oops, sorry, I didn't mean to say something about, you know, because your sister died. I just meant . . ."

"It's okay," I said.

"Oh my gosh, did your sister die of cancer? Or peanuts? Because I didn't—"

"No," I said. "Neither of those."

"Oh, good," Dorin said. "I mean, not good but—or puking?"

"No," I said again.

"I always say stupid stuff," Dorin said. "When I'm nervous, especially."

"Don't we all?" I said.

"I don't know," Dorin said.

"We do," Sienna said. "Everybody does."

"Oh, thank you," Dorin gushed. "So much. That's very reassuring and nice of you. Both. Thanks. You're the nicest girls in school."

I shrugged. "We just don't want you to puke."

"Oh," Dorin said.

"Just kidding," I said.

Dorin smiled, even though the bright-red patches on her pale cheeks glowed like fresh burns. "I'm so sorry you can't buy that tort. You really belong together."

"We should go," Sienna said.

I handed the tortoise back to Dorin.

"Yeah," Dorin said, more to the tortoise than to me. "Have fun."

"Your hair looks cute," Sienna said. "It really does."

"And you're awesome, donating it like that," I added.

"Riley was just being mean because she's mean," Sienna said.

"And had gotten some disappointing news," I said. "And she took it out on the first person she saw. It had nothing to do with you."

Sienna started to ask, "What news—"

"Are you just saying that?" Dorin interrupted, luckily. "Just kidding?"

"No, I'm also meaning it," I said.

Dorin got busy putting the tortoise I loved back into the tank. I turned around so I wouldn't have to look at anybody, and walked up the steps ahead of Sienna.

"Hello," the parrot called to us.

"Good-bye," we both said back.

"Hello," the parrot insisted as we left. "Hello!"

15

SECRETS

I once found a small blue box in my mother's sock drawer. I held it in my hand for a minute before I dared to open it. It looked like a box of stationery, nothing I wouldn't be allowed to see. But why would Mom have a box of stationery hidden at the bottom of her sock drawer? I tried to just put it back without looking but couldn't. I opened it.

It was full of pictures. Bret and Mom, Bret and Dad, Bret and Mom and Dad, Bret and Grandma and Pops, just Bret and just Bret and just Bret, all ages, up to seven.

I'd been looking for a pair of cozy socks. I was in third grade. I was eight.

It felt like I'd stumbled onto a pirate's treasure chest. Or maybe something secret and scary. In the red album next to the couch, I'm in most of the photos. In the stationery box hidden under Mom's socks, there were zero pictures of me.

There are lots of pictures of me in frames around the apartment. It's not that.

I sat there looking at every picture while Grandma, who was babysitting, was in the bathroom. After the flush, I quickly put them back, in the same order, and tucked them under Mom's socks, my heart pounding. I didn't take a cozy pair for myself. I closed the drawer and tiptoed out fast.

Sometimes when Mom and Dad are out, I look again. Not that often. I always feel bad about myself when I sneak in there, like I've violated Mom's privacy.

I tell Sienna pretty much everything, but I never told her or anybody about that. Not sure why. I guess everybody has secrets.

And not just about why Riley was actually mad, or a recipe for red velvet cupcakes.

16

SERIOUSLY

While the fourth batch of cupcakes was baking, Sienna's phone buzzed.

AJ.

We stared at each other, then down at the phone, then at each other again. He was asking if the math test was tomorrow.

"What should I say?" she asked me. She didn't even know I had experience with AJ asking if the math test was tomorrow.

"Say yeah," I suggested. "Because, yeah."

"Yeah or yes?"

"Either?"

"I don't want to sound stupid, but I don't want to sound, you know, annoyed."

Good thing I am not the one who has to flirt. What had I answered when he asked me? Nope, nope, nope. No backsies. "Maybe *yeah*, and then put an emoji?"

"Okay," Sienna said. Finding the right emoji was a project. Then she hit send and we waited, staring at the phone, for AJ to respond.

Nothing.

Nothing.

Sienna and I sat, her quiet phone between us, wondering how do other girls know how to flirt? The Loud Crowd, for example. They've been flirting and going out with one another since, like, sixth grade. Michaela and David seem so happy and maybe even in love, like they're seventeen or something. Maybe she and Beth, who flirts with all the guys, no problem, could tutor us, or there could be a class on flirting instead of volleyball?

Because, really: When is volleyball going to be useful in life?

On the other hand, I had to point out, maybe the fact that Sienna was good at volleyball in fact *was* helpful in getting AJ's attention. Maybe *good at volleyball* is what boys actually like? A lot of the Loud Crowd is on the volleyball team with Sienna.

Sienna had stopped talking, I noticed. She looked miserable.

"How cute was that tortoise?" I said, to change the topic.

"Super cute." Sienna smiled, relieved to get back to normal conversation about tortoises and my birthday and the bake sale. "How sad is it that so many kids own zero books and have nothing to eat tonight for dinner?" she said. "When our big problems are how to flirt and too many cupcakes for available Tupperware carriers?"

"Seriously," I agreed. But we both kept looking at that phone, silent and dark between us. The house phone rang. We both jolted back, confused.

It was Sienna's doorman, calling up to say my mom was downstairs. I told him I'd come down and meet her, because right then their nanny, Manuela, was opening their front door. She was coming back from Chelsea Piers with Sienna's twin brothers, so things were chaotic enough. I can't always tell the twins apart, except when they are together, and even then, they are in constant motion, so sometimes, like suddenly in the kitchen, they just look like a boy-infused blur. They immediately started playing catch with the two eggs we had left over from all our batches.

Manuela was yelling, "Those are eggs, not balls, *gorditos*! Put them down! In the carton, not on the floor!" while I argued with my mom through the doorman ("No, really, please tell her I will come right down!").

"I gotta go," I told Sienna.

"Take me with you," she whispered.

"*Cupcakes!*" one of the twins started chanting.

"*Cupcakes?*" the other twin shouted. "I need *cupcakes*!"

Distracted by the cupcakes, the boys abandoned their eggs, which rolled in opposite directions across the counter, just missing colliding in front of one platter of cupcakes. Manuela somehow caught both eggs as they rolled off the counter. She is really coordinated and fast.

"No cupcakes yet," Manuela bargained with the boys while holding one egg in each hand as if they were grenades. "Go wash your hands first. With soap! I want to smell soap!" she yelled, flashing us a game grin and then following the boys out and down the hall toward their bathroom.

Sienna was shaking her head, muttering, "Crazy monsters," while we put the two cupcakes we'd made especially for them on the purple glass dessert plates I love from their dish cabinet. We always make the twins special treats. This time we had decorated one cupcake for each of them with their initials in sprinkles.

We could hear them in the hall bathroom, having a loud splashy time of it, while I gathered up my stuff. Sienna's apartment is huge and always spotless except wherever the boys have just been, and matchingly decorated, all of which is very unlike my book-filled cozy mismatchy home. But like mine, it's shoes-off, so I'd have to grab my sneakers on my way out. They were way down near the door. The door is very far from the kitchen. Sienna's apartment has stairs in it, up to her parents' room, and a huge private deck overlooking the park.

I was about to say bye when her phone buzzed again: **Ugh.**

Sienna and I stared at those three letters AJ had texted back.

"What does that even mean?" Sienna asked. "*Ugh*?"

"He's not in the mood for a math test tomorrow?"

"What should I say?"

I turned off the oven and opened the door. The cupcakes looked great, the best batch yet.

"You don't mind frosting these alone?"

"No, it's fine, but, Gracie, what do I say to AJ? What's the right answer to *Ugh*?"

"I don't know. Maybe just: *Yeah*?"

"Again?"

"Good point." I looked at her phone. No brilliant responses were occurring to me. "I gotta go or my mom will come up." Her brothers were rumbling toward us.

"You have to tell me what to say," Sienna said. Her cute face scrunched up all sad and adorable. "This is too weird! I've been friends with AJ since forever, but now it's all awkward just texting about a stupid math test and it's your fault, Gracie!"

"My fault?"

"Yes! Fully! If you hadn't told me that he—"

"Okay, sure, true," I said.

"Gracie," she begged. Her frown got all huge and blobfish-like. She really is adorable. Good choice, AJ.

"You should just take a selfie and send that. Your face is so cute and worried."

"You're the worst!"

"Me?" I asked. "I'm the best! No insulting ourselves!"

"True," she groaned. "But . . ."

We started laughing a little. I looked at the phone again. "Maybe say, *Seriously*."

"Okay, yeah," Sienna said, brightening. "That's good."

"I'm a genius."

"You are. Okay. *Seriously*." She typed it. "Yeah?" She showed it to me.

"Yeah," I said, and pressed send for her.

"Ahhh!" She dropped the phone onto the counter like it was too hot to hold.

"No, it's good. You can just, like, bat it back at him, whatever he says."

"Yeah?" she asked.

"Just like that!" I shrugged. "That way, you don't, you know, get out too far ahead of it. Of the, you know, flirting."

"Ugh," she moaned. "Everything was normal until today."

"You got this. You're great. He already likes you, so . . ."

"My hands are shaking!" She held them out to me.

"Do you like him back, then, you think?"

She shrugged one shoulder and blinked her dark eyes twice. "I guess?"

"You can remind him to bring money for the bake sale, if you have to say something else," I suggested.

"Oh, that's good! Thanks."

"Any time." I grabbed my shoes from the pretty iron shoe rack and called good-byes to Manuela and the boys. "Good luck!" I added to Sienna.

"Keep your phone charged and with you," she said, leaning against the doorframe, one foot balanced on the other. "This is your fault and you have to help me!"

"You know I always have your back," I said, waving without turning around.

"Yeah, I do know," I heard her say as the door between us closed.

It was suddenly quiet, out in the cool carpeted hall. I pushed the elevator button and checked my phone. Nothing. No texts from anybody wondering if there was a math test tomorrow or whatever. Sure. I wasn't expecting anything, just checking. I put the phone into my pocket as I stepped onto the fancy elevator. I had it to myself. Good. Long day. Better that I didn't pour out my whole story to Sienna about what Riley had said to me. Sienna had enough going on. My job is to be sunshine for her, too.

Good thing I am so sunshiney!

I pressed the button for the lobby and sagged against the back wall as the doors slid silently closed, and felt myself standing still but still sinking down, down, down.

17

SOMETHING GOOD

Down in Sienna's elegant lobby, my mom was frowning the way she does when she's worried about something and doesn't want to show it. Or sometimes when she's trying not to smile. Hard to tell.

"How was your day?" she asked.

"Fine," I lied. We both called good-bye and thank you to the doorman, who clicked the magic button to auto-open the door for us. "What's up?"

"Nothing. Your day was good?"

"Sure," I lied again. "Is something—Why are you frowning?"

"I'm not," she lied. We are quite a pair. "Do you have a lot of homework?"

"Not a ton," I said. A truth! Yay!

"How was your day?"

"Did somebody call you and tell you I had a bad day?"

"No!" She laughed, as if that were an impossibility, my having a bad day.

When I got home, Dad was there. Usually he stays at his office late on Thursday nights. Again I asked what was going on.

"Come down the hall," Dad suggested.

"Am I in trouble?" I asked.

"Did you do something bad?" Mom asked, like she was teasing.

Uh, yeah. Kind of. Did school call home to tell my parents about me telling off Riley? I was just trying to defend Dorin! And myself!

Oh, Bret, why do you have to be dead instead of warning me what they are up to?

I kicked off my shoes, dropped my backpack inside my bedroom door, and started down the hall, asking, "Seriously, what?"

And then I saw it. On the kitchen counter. A huge blue Tupperware bin and, inside it, the speed-demon tortoise from the funky pet store just past Ninety-Ninth. I recognized her immediately. Partly, okay, because she was desperately trying to dig her way down and out of the bin, through the brown mulchlike stuff in the base of the container. But partly just because, well, I just recognized her.

"What . . ." I managed to ask, my mouth hanging open. "What is . . ."

I turned my head and then my eyes away from the speed-demon tortoise and toward my parents, who were standing together in the kitchen, smiling expectantly.

"But . . ." I couldn't even formulate a sentence.

"Happy birthday," Mom said, clapping her hands a little in front of her neck.

"Do you like it?" Dad asked.

"Is it . . . Is she really . . . She's mine?"

They nodded.

And I managed to hug them both, so tight, before I even picked up the speed-demon tortoise.

My tortoise.

Mine.

18

HEAD-DOWN IN A BOOT

Could there actually be such a thing as love at first sight?

I know I told my parents that a tortoise would not just be like a pet rock, but maybe I had been a little bit worried that having a tortoise might be like having a pet rock.

If I ever got one. Which I never thought could happen.

But now . . .

This tortoise just killed me. When I took her out of the bin and put her gently onto the floor, she marched up the hall like she was on patrol, and then back down again. We gave her a string bean, which she chased after like a slow-motion cheetah wearing a mobile home. She was so funny. The pet store guy told my parents when they went to pick her up that the tortoise could have one string bean, occasionally, as a treat. There's too much protein for her otherwise. Too much protein in a string bean.

Crazy amounts of information, but what I really wanted to know was: What finally convinced them to get this tortoise, and when, and how did they know she was the One?

"Sometimes you just know," Dad said. "And then you think: *Of course. Of course.*"

"Okay," I said. "If you say so."

"It's true," Dad said.

Mom kept taking pictures and videos, and cracking up with me every time the tortoise went sprinting around, her legs moving so fast, she ended up doing clonking belly flops onto the hardwood floor. Dad suggested naming her either Champ or Hildegard. Mom said either Plautus or Lightning, because of a play she likes—I can't remember the name—that had a tortoise in it named both of those names. I said, "Or maybe Thelonious," which Dad was completely on board with, but Mom said Thelonious was maybe a mouthful. "Completely up to you," Dad said. "Name her whatever you want."

I gave him a hug and then gave Mom a big one too. "This is the best birthday present anybody ever got," I said. They were smiling such happy smiles. Then my tortoise bit my toe. It hurt a tiny bit but mostly just surprised me.

"Maybe I'll name her Jaws," I said. "Or Maniac."

I Snapchatted a shot of myself next to the tortoise to a bunch of my friends, with hearts drawn all around us.

In about five seconds Emmett responded, a selfie with his mouth hanging open and blue question marks over his eyes.

I texted that he should come up and see. Since he lives just four flights down in my building, he was knocking on our door by the time I got to it.

He agreed with me right away that this was the most amazing tortoise in the history of tortoises, and also that we needed to race her against his pet rabbit because *tortoise and hare*. We bet a 16 Handles frozen yogurt with as many toppings as you want.

"I so obviously win," I boasted. "Have you never read Aesop?"

"Yeah, but they call it a fable for a reason," Emmett said.

"Marketing?"

"Yeah," he conceded. "Fully. Fricking marketing."

He pulled his phone out of his pocket and stared at the screen.

"What?" I asked.

"Nothing. AJ."

My phone buzzed. It was Sienna, saying: **were you completely surprised?**

YES! I texted back. **you knew? were you in on this?**

maybe . . . she texted back.

"What's up?" Emmett asked.

"Sienna," I said. "I think she was somehow in on the whole get-the-tortoise thing with my parents."

"Did she say that?"

"Were you in on it too?"

"I was at opera all afternoon," he said, but with such an innocent face, it made me completely suspicious. "But hey, I wanted to say, about what you were saying to Riley?"

Both of our phones buzzed again, so we groaned at each other and dealt with our separate issues. Sienna said AJ had texted her, asking her what she's doing this weekend. *Ack!* What should she say?

"Sorry—what were you saying?" I asked Emmett instead of answering Sienna.

He shoved his phone back into his pocket. "Nothing. I should go, I guess."

"Oh, okay," I said. "Was that your mom?" His mom hates when he doesn't respond right away, like mine.

"Nah, she's at the art gallery." His phone buzzed again. He ignored it. "Did you name it?"

"Name what?" I asked. "I think that's you buzzing again. . ."

"Your tortoise," he said.

I told him all the choices we were considering. He liked Lightning and Hamburger best but said, "Let's see which one she comes to, if you call her."

"Great idea," I said. "Wait! Where is she?"

We jumped up and started looking around. I'd had the

tortoise for what, twenty minutes? And I'd already lost her. Wow, that's gotta be a record. Maybe my parents had the right idea with not letting me have a pet after all.

"Am I the worst tortoise person ever? I had this image of myself as, like, you know, decent at—"

"No way. You're the world champion tortoise person," Emmett said, peeking into my bedroom for her.

"Or at least not the worst?" I bargained, flopping onto my floor to look under my bed. Lots of books, some socks, some mystery things, possibly underwear, oops, embarrassing. No tort.

"Absolutely," Emmett agreed. "I'd put money on you not being the worst."

"Thanks, Emmett. That means a lot to me."

"You're welcome."

I looked behind my door. Just a sweatshirt on the floor. The soft red hoodie I love. Emmett has the same one. I hung it on the hook and went back into the hall. "A, not the worst ever," I asked him, "are you saying? Or B, not the worst tortoise person currently alive?"

"No," Emmett said, peeking behind my laundry hamper. "Definitely A. Assuming you didn't lose the tortoise already, because I'm pretty sure we'll find her eventually, I see you going all the way to the, you know, World Series Super Bowl of Not-Worst Tortoise People Ever this year. Final Four, at least."

"You're just saying that because you want free tickets to the Tortoise World Series with . . . Oh!"

"What?"

Emmett looked where I was pointing, toward the front door. There, poking out of the top of one of my dad's boots, was the butt of my new tortoise.

The rest of her was plunged deep inside.

Emmett and I both doubled over laughing before I could even rescue her. I reached in and lifted her carefully out. She looked at me, world-weary and resigned.

"Hey, pal," I said. "What were you looking for?"

"Oh, nothing," Emmett answered for the tortoise.

"Rough first day?" I asked her.

"Nah," Emmett answered for her. "Sometimes you just end up head-down in a boot, you know?"

"Story of my life," I said, and placed my tortoise down gently on the floor.

Emmett and I watched her head toward the kitchen. His phone buzzed in his pocket. Mine buzzed in mine.

"Maybe Lightning," he said. "Suits her."

"Yeah, it does."

"Or Flight Plan."

"That could be her nickname."

"Or Dash," he said. "Maybe Flash?"

I laughed. "Lightning, and her nickname could be Flash?"

"Perfect." His phone buzzed again. He said, "I should—"

"Yeah, okay, later," I said. "Thanks!"

"Anytime somebody's head-down in a boot up here," Emmett said, "just call me!"

"Better keep your phone with you," I said, "at all times, in that case."

I heard him laughing in the stairwell behind the closed door while I followed my tort down the hall, challenging her to a race, ignoring for one more second the texts coming in from my best friend, asking for flirtation help.

19

TESTING, TESTING

Riley came early, as we were setting up for the bake sale. I took a deep breath.

"Hi!" She smiled at Sienna and me so sweetly, I wondered for a second if it was her sister, Amelia, instead of actual Riley.

"Hi," we both answered.

"What are you raising money for this time?" she asked.

"Kids who have no books," I said.

"Very noble," Riley said, and handed me a crisp five-dollar bill. "It's so cute how 'noble' you two are."

"Thanks," I said, unconvinced she meant it as a compliment.

"You can take ten cupcakes," Sienna said quietly.

"Oh, I don't eat that stuff," Riley said, fluffing her hair. "It's a donation. For your 'cause.'"

"Listen, Riley," I said, still holding her money in my hand. "About yesterday."

"Don't be embarrassed," Riley said. "Everybody knows you get loud sometimes. Let's just forget it. I already forgot all about it; don't worry. But—Sienna!"

"What?" Sienna asked.

"I heard about you and AJ!"

"You did?"

"Gracie told me yesterday!" She winked at me. "That's so cute. Have you ever gone out with anybody?"

"No."

"Oh. Hmm. Or you, either—right, Gracie?"

"No."

"Don't worry," Riley said. "I'll help you, Sienna. We all will. We all think you two make an adorable couple. Oh!"

AJ was walking in, his long legs lunging through the entryway.

"Did you bring money to support their 'noble' cause?" Riley asked AJ.

"Oops," AJ said. "I forgot."

"No worries," Riley said, and handed him five dollars. "Here! Support them!"

AJ gave me the five and then handed out seven cupcakes to whoever wanted them as they came in, but meanwhile ate/inhaled three himself. He said they were great, which made Sienna smile but then look down and rearrange the rows of cupcakes we had left.

I told him there was frosting on his chin. He thanked me, wiping it off.

When he got to school, Emmett paid his dollar for two cupcakes and chose the most misshapen ones on the table. He said it was because he likes them weird-looking, but I think maybe it's because he thought nobody else would buy them. But who really knows what somebody else actually likes and why? Maybe Emmett just has odd taste.

Then we had to hurry and get rid of the trash, to move on with the day. I tucked the $47.50 we'd made into the envelope I'd brought for it, which I'd give to Dad, who'd write a check for it to send to firstbook.org for me. He usually adds a little to the tally. "Just rounding up," he always says.

I shoved the stash deep into my backpack, and then we ran up to math, where the test had already started. "Sorry, sorry," I said, and got to it. We all grumbled after, but really, the math test was fine.

The awkwardness at lunch was less fine.

On our way there, Sienna finally whispered to me, "You told Riley that I like AJ?"

"No." I shook my head. "That's not . . ."

"You're the only one who knew."

"I didn't . . ."

"It's okay," Sienna said. "It's just—"

"Sienna, I . . . That's not how—"

"I get it," Sienna said, sitting down at our usual spot. I sat next to her. "You were trying to not fight with her or whatever, over the Dorin thing, but . . ."

"No," I said. "That's not—"

"Let's talk about it later," she whispered as Emmett and AJ sat down across from us. We ate our sandwiches in grim silence, no eye contact, no chatting, no smiling. We all used to have so much fun. Like, last week.

Time flies. I never fully got that expression before today. *Tempus fugit.* Sounds like ancient Latin cursing. It sort of is, I guess.

Because now that *tempus* has *fugit*, everything is awkward and nobody can even eat or talk. Only Riley was chatting. Flipping her hair around. She had sat down on the other side of Sienna and kept bumping her with her shoulder, trying to include both Sienna and AJ in her boring conversation. But Sienna and AJ just sat there, not responding. Nobody was responding that much, not even Harrison, who is usually Riley's best audience even though she ignores him, so ultimately even she stopped saying things, and didn't eat more than three sections of the sad little tangerine that was her whole lunch.

AJ left half his sandwich. AJ. Until today nothing had ever stopped him from gobbling up everything. During gym activities, I mentioned it to Emmett, to ask if he thought that was weird.

"Deeply," Emmett said. "Last month AJ was sleeping over one night and we went to the kitchen to get a snack at, like, one a.m., and AJ fell asleep while eating pad Thai takeout left over from dinner."

"While actively eating?"

"Yes," Emmett insisted. "He literally fell asleep sitting at my kitchen table, but he just kept eating."

"Seriously?" I managed to ask. We were fake-playing basketball, meaning Emmett and I were mostly wandering around as far from the ball as possible. Luckily on the same team. Avoiding the obvious topics of me versus Riley or Sienna plus AJ.

"He finished the whole container, fast asleep."

"No way."

"I took a video," Emmett said.

"That is hilarious."

"Show you later, if you want. You around after school?"

"Yeah," I said. "Playing with the tort. Lightning. Or do you think I should change her name to Tempus?"

"Tempus?"

"You know," I said, and had one of those instant full-body sweat attacks I sometimes get when I know I am in the process of saying the nerdiest possible thing, so shut up, but Emmett was standing there in front of me, all cute, his head tilted to the side, his dark eyes latched on to mine. "*Tempus fugit*?" I said, hating myself. "Time, you know, flies. Because she's so fast and, like, never stops. Get it? Forget it. *Boooo!* Could I be any dorkier?"

He smiled. "That is the truest thing about time."

"What is?"

"That it *fugits*."

I smiled back at him. "Yeah. The truest thing for sure."

"*Tempus* just ceaselessly *fugits* and nothing we can do about it."

"Emmett! Gracie!" Awesome Ms. Washington yelled. "Did you forget you're in the middle of a basketball game?"

"Yup!" Emmett yelled back.

"Is there a basketball game?" I yelled. "We were wondering why everybody keeps running around here!"

"It's kind of annoying actually," Emmett said.

"A little hustle!" Awesome Ms. Washington yelled. "At least get out of the way?"

"Sure!" I yelled. "No problem!"

"But Lightning is good, I think," Emmett said after we'd jogged to the far corner of the court. "Really good."

"My mom really likes it," I said.

"Do you?"

"Yeah," I said. "It suits her, don't you think?"

"It does. But I'm still calling her Flight Plan anyway. Or Tempus, maybe. I'll come up; we can try out all the nicknames. I have opera tonight, but before that?"

"Sure. So—he was actually sleep-eating? AJ?" My mouth went completely dry as it said his name, so I had to stop avoiding the ball to hack out some coughs.

"You okay?" Emmett asked.

I nodded. "Just choking. Sometimes I choke on, you know, air."

"Sure," Emmett said.

"AJ doesn't even choke on pad Thai when he eats it while sleeping?"

"Just one of his many skills, I guess," Emmett said. "We can't all be AJ."

More choking from me.

Awesome Ms. Washington told Emmett to walk me to the water fountain. Hallelujah. Fake-playing basketball is exhausting.

20

PLOTTING

Emmett looked at me quizzically as he was leaving school. I shrugged, not ready to walk home yet, even though I'd gotten out the front door ahead of him. I was bunched up against the outside wall of school with Sienna and the Loud Crowd, plotting.

Emmett shrugged back and walked alone to the corner.

Watching him wait for the walk sign, I wished I could just go with him. We'd walk home together, joking about whatever, saying hi to the homeless woman who sits outside the bank and usually asks us if we're studying hard. Maybe we'd pause to look at the stuff on the table of the guy on our corner. He has really nice jewelry and some unfortunate-looking hats for sale there. Emmett and I always plan which of the hugie hats with the nylon or mesh see-through tops to buy for each other someday.

But no. There's not really a way to leave your best friend plotting with the most popular girls and instead go do normal stuff like chat with the friendly homeless woman and fake-choose silly hats. No. There are rules against treason like that when you are a girl and in eighth grade and somebody likes somebody.

"You have to make sure you wait at least five minutes before you text him back," Beth was whispering to Sienna. "You don't want to look overeager."

"I'm not," Sienna said. "Overeager? I'm so not."

"That's all Beth is saying," Riley said. "You don't want to look desperate."

"Do I seem desperate?" Sienna asked me.

"No," I said honestly. "Desperate to . . . what?"

"To be asked out," Riley said patiently, like I was the slowest person ever, then turned away from dummy me to smile at Sienna. "When do you think he'll ask you?"

Sienna's eyes got even bigger than usual, which made her look particularly manga-ish. "I don't know," she whispered. "I don't even know if he's . . . How would I know?"

"Maybe he'll text you to ask you out tonight," Michaela suggested.

"You think?" Sienna asked.

They all looked at me.

"What?" I asked. "Why are you all looking at me? How would I know?"

They turned back to Sienna. "You'd say yes, right?" Michaela asked her. "If AJ texted you tonight and asked you out? Not like on a date, obviously, but . . ."

"Oh yikes, a *date*?" Sienna asked.

"Right but not," Michaela assured her. "Just *out*."

Sienna shrugged. "I guess so."

"Okay, then." Riley smiled calmly at Sienna and then at me. "That's all you need to tell Emmett, then, Gracie. Just say that you can't tell him how you know, but that if AJ texts Sienna tonight and asks her out, she'd say yes. And then he'll text her!"

Michaela and Beth both nodded their agreement. "She's right," Michaela said.

"But wait five minutes before responding," Beth told Sienna. "Set a timer."

"You want me to?" I asked Sienna. "Tell Emmett that?"

She started to shrug but then nodded a tiny bit. "If . . . I mean, you don't have to."

"Oh, no!" I protested. "I'm totally happy to, if you want me to!"

"This is so exciting," Riley whispered. "I mean, you're actually pretty, Sienna. It's a little weird you haven't gone out with anybody yet."

Okay, I thought, *time for me to go home now*.

"Ouch, Riley," Michaela said. "Anyway, AJ's never gone out with anybody yet either, so . . ."

"Which is adorable, for both of them, is all I'm saying," Riley whispered. "But he might be a little awkward about getting things started, so we'll have to, you know, set it all up for him so he'll do it right."

Beth shook her head a tiny bit, like, *Yeah, Riley is horrible, but what can you do?*

"Don't worry," Riley said. "This is how we always do it. Right?"

"It is," Michaela said, shrugging.

"Just trust us," Riley said. "And it'll all work out."

Sienna winced.

"We should go back in for volleyball," Michaela said. "Come on, Sienna."

"I should go too," I said. "I have to, you know, feed my tortoise. Super busy."

"Don't forget!" Riley called after me.

"Forget what?"

"Ugh, Gracie. Tell Emmett," Riley yell-whispered to me. "To tell . . . you know who . . . about . . . he should text her? And what she'll say if he—"

"Oh. Right," I said. "Sure."

"Then text us all and tell us what he says!" Beth yelled.

I nodded.

"Maybe this will all happen before Gracie's party tomorrow!" Riley yelled.

Unfortunately Dorin was trudging out of school just as Riley yelled that toward me. Dorin looked from Riley to me. She tilted her head, then swallowed hard and watched her feet walking toward Amsterdam, away from where I was waiting for the light to change, and also away from where she normally walks, which is down Broadway. Guess she decided to take the long way around, to avoid me and the party she just found out about and learned in the same second that she hadn't been invited to.

The homeless woman wasn't in front of the bank and I didn't even say hi to Jewelry/Wacky Hat Man on my way home. That's how bad I felt.

21

RULE OF THUMBS

me: hey so you wanna come up and help me teach this tortoise some supercoolio tricks?

EMMETT: Yeah, maybe a summersault? And also I can show you that video of AJ sleep-eating.

me: excellent. I was thinking we'd start with a cartwheel but sure, a somersault is good too. speaking of AJ . . . he should prob ask out Sienna

EMMETT: It's such a funny video. You are gonna crack up, but I have to be back down here to eat by 5 bc my call is at 6:15, so wait, WHAT?

me: u coming up?

EMMETT: Um, yeah, but what? AJ should ask out Sienna? Not sure why you're telling me . . . ???

me: u shd text him that he should ask her out

EMMETT: Haha, k. I'll just text him his marching orders then be up in a sec.

me: awesome

EMMETT: Wait, r u serious? This is too weird.

me: hahahaha idk not my idea just passing along a message yk?

EMMETT: Oh. So what am I telling him then?

me: I guess . . . just . . . just say that if he asks Sienna out she'd prob say yes?

EMMETT: Okay. Just that? "If you ask Sienna out, she'd prob say yes"???

me: maybe?

EMMETT: Okay. This is srsly the randomest text I've ever sent. Sending it . . .

me: maybe also: you should ask her out?

EMMETT: ME? WHAT???

me: no tell AJ! that HE shd ask Sienna out

EMMETT: Um, okay, now you want me to text him, "You should ask Sienna out"? REALLY???

me: IDK

EMMETT: Maybe YOU should just text AJ?

me: not it

EMMETT: ☹

me: anyway I was told YOU should text him

EMMETT: Oh, well, then I guess I better get to it. We are just cogs in this machine.

me: haha yeah exactly what we are: the cogs.
we could be a band

EMMETT: That's totally our band name: THE COGS. We should learn some instruments.

me: YES! so are you on the stairs yet? I think the tort is napping. should I wake her up?

EMMETT: Yeah, texting AJ then omw—tell that lazy tort to get ready to be COACHED.

me: kk

RILEY: Gracie! Update us!

me: I told Emmett and he's texting AJ

SIENNA: right now?

me: yeah

SIENNA: is it stupid tho if I already know? bc now what I am supposed to do? just sit here and wait to see if he texts me? isn't that kind of 100 years ago ish?

me: yes

RILEY: NO!

SIENNA: bc honestly, I could just ask him out if I wanna go out w him, which do I even? I mean, I like him but . . .

RILEY: If you say no now, we will all look like such idiots, Sienna.

MICHAELA: We? Riley, stop.

RILEY: Well, mostly Sienna hahahaha, jk. Lol.

SIENNA: maybe I should just . . . ugh, idk.

me: are you guys still at practice?

BETH: just left!!! short one today—like me! Yay shorties!!!

SIENNA: omg, he just texted me.

RILEY: WHAT DID HE SAY?????

SIENNA: how's it goin?

me: are you just randomly asking us how it's going or is that what he texted you?

SIENNA: :-/

RILEY: What did you say back? Do you want my car to swing around and pick you up?

SIENNA: what? no!

I haven't texted back anything yet! I am waiting five minutes!

what should I say? "fine"?

me: isn't he at soccer or whatever?

SIENNA: baseball.

me: so maybe say how's baseball?

SIENNA: that's good. I like that.

me: I am such a poet. I have endless savior fairer

SIENNA: ????

me: autocorrect. hahahaha. savoir faire

RILEY: Gracie, just stop. Sienna is trying to do something important.

BETH: I thought How's baseball was a good idea.

MICHAELA: same

SIENNA: me too. thanks, Gracie. you're the bombalicious.

me: if the bombalicious is cake, I so am. I am the cake. such panache

SIENNA: panache is the best. that's the stuff between the cake layers, right?

me: yup! chocolate panache. yum

SIENNA: so wait, what should I say, then? exactly?

me: how about: fine, you? how's baseball going?

SIENNA: perfect. I'm literally copying and pasting that.

me: I'm honored. it's practically like I'm texting him

SIENNA: I wish.

me: dtuyikbfc

RILEY: What does that even stand for, Gracie? Don't Tie Up Your . . . ???

me: nothing sorry dropped my phone

MICHAELA: hahahaha! GL gotta run bye girls! xoxox

BETH: text me when you get home, Michaela! <3

RILEY: Love you guys! Sienna: text him and then tell us what he says.

SIENNA: kk

EMMETT: Should I bring Fluff up?

me: hold on I'll ask

me: My mom says no not yet let the tort get used to being here for a week or two before we subject her to racing the rabbit sorry

EMMETT: Good call, good call, but no extra training sessions for the tort, bc, unfair.

me: rats foiled again. did you tell AJ?

EMMETT: Yeah.

me: is he

EMMETT: Is he . . . ???

RILEY: Did he respond yet?

SIENNA: nope

RILEY: Don't panic.

SIENNA: why would you say don't panic? I was not panicking until you said don't panic.

EMMETT: Gracie?

me: sorry we're a little freaked out on this end

EMMETT: Yeah, a little this side too.

me: really?

RILEY: Is your phone def working? Are you on the subway or something?

SIENNA: YES, it's working and NO, I'm walking home! still nothing back from AJ yet. should I say something else?

BETH: Don't double text!

SIENNA: okay, good advice. maybe I have to stop at Starbucks and get a Frappuccino bc I might pass out. this is so much.

RILEY: OTOH, maybe say something about what you're doing (don't mention the Frappuccino :-/ oink, oink!), so he doesn't think you're just sitting around waiting for him to text back. You wanna seem busy. Like you have a life.

SIENNA: I do have a life!

me: what are you doing?

SIENNA: staring at my phone, waiting for him to text me back. I hate myself now.

me: nope nope nope

SIENNA: oops.

me: maybe text him something like I am *not* sitting around watching videos on YouTube FYI. I so much have a life. wanted you to know

RILEY: Gracie, just stop.

me: or something like that. yk, keep it funny and normal

MICHAELA: Ha! I like hey I'm not watching YouTube just wanted you to know

RILEY: Yeah, that's good, actually. Not too funny. Just flirty. And busy. Boys like it when you are busy. With fun things. But not jokey jokey, ykwim? Maybe tell him you are about to go for a run or something. Boys like sporty girls. No offense, Gracie.

me: what? me? how did I get dragged into this?

RILEY: I wasn't being critical. I know you get sensitive.

me: um none taken?

SIENNA: AJ just texted back. I don't know whether to be ecstatic or upset.

me: why? what did he say?

SIENNA: here it is. I screenshotted it:

Hope your well, this has put a smile on my face.

me: hmmm

SIENNA: what do you think?

me: maybe neither ecstatic nor upset?

RILEY: No, that seems awesome! Now wait him out. Make HIM double text. Pretend you're busy.

SIENNA: I AM busy. analyzing.

here's my analysis:

bad: two grammatical errors.

good: HE SAID I MADE HIM SMILE. ☺

bad: omg, who am I?

bad: almost stepped off the curb into traffic, texting this.

BETH: Maybe just text him back a smiley face, but after seven minutes. Set a timer.

me: maybe don't text and walk, dude? also maybe text him his text back with edits? I read on the internet that boys totally love being corrected

RILEY: Um, no.

me: I was kidding!

me: Sienna?

me: Sienna? I was so just kidding, you know that right? except about the texting-while-walking

me: quad-texting. I am soooo cooool

EMMETT: I'm knocking at your door. Are you in there? I don't want to ring the bell and wake up your tort if she's still sleeping. . . .

EMMETT: Gracie? You didn't press the secret don't-automatically-lock-thing on your door so I can't get in. . . .

me: the what?

EMMETT: I'm at your door.

me: sorry coming I accidentally threw my phone at the wall because omg people are so weird and then I had to get it out from behind my bed 1 sec hi

EMMETT: Hi.

22

BEWARE OF WOLF

"What automatic thing so it doesn't lock?" I asked, opening the door.

Emmett touched one of the many random brass things I'd never paid any attention to before on the narrowest side plane of the door and clicked it up. "Go out," he said.

"Really?" I stepped into the hall, and Emmett closed my own apartment door behind me, leaving me alone out there. I stood there in my socks, feeling weirdly lonely and abandoned.

"Now open it," he said, from inside my apartment.

I turned the knob and, for the first time ever, my door opened without a key.

"What?"

He smiled, his eyes crinkling up all glittery.

"If your opera and comp sci and journalism careers don't work out," I said, "you could totally have a life of crime ahead of you."

"Gotta keep my options open," he said, and flicked the secret switch back to lock.

"I totally had no idea that existed," I said, clicking it up and down a few times myself.

"Daphne had some trouble keeping track of her keys last year," Emmett said. "So if my mom was gonna be out . . ."

"And nobody would know, so, safe, still."

"Exactly."

"The more you know . . ."

"Hey, so I have an idea," he said.

"Speaking of brilliant?"

"Yes," he said. "We could walk down Broadway to Lincoln Center together, and then you could take the subway back up while I go to opera."

"Why would I do that?"

"We could eat the whole way down. I have to eat dinner early anyway. There's that 16 Handles at Ninety-Eighth Street, and you know you're gonna owe me one when Fluff beats Lightning in a race, so you could get an early jump on—"

"Never. Gonna. Happen."

"Ha!" Never Gonna Happen is kind of an inside joke with my family and his. "Thing is," he said, "most things people say are Never Gonna Happen eventually do happen."

"Sure. I'm still not buying you a 16 Handles in advance."

"Fine, fine. We'll split it."

"Your mom lets you get 16 Handles for dinner?"

"No," he said. "But why doesn't she? Frozen yogurt is probably healthy. Isn't it just very cold yogurt?"

"Good point," I said. "Plus, they have fruit toppings you can put on, not just smashed-up cookies and hot fudge and Fruity Pebbles like a normal person."

"Exactly. Or Gray's Papaya has hot dogs, which probably are some percentage made of food. In addition to whatever other disgusting—don't think about it—deliciousness is in them. Plus, all the fruit stands and bodegas. A feast, I'm telling you."

"Sounds awesome," I said. "Okay, I'm in."

"If you're not hungry, we don't have to eat. We could just walk. My mom always packs me a big sandwich to eat during the second intermission. I get really hungry in this opera."

"Big part?"

"Kind of," he admitted, blushing a bit. "Also, really sweaty."

"Ha!" I said. "I am the gold medalist of sweaty."

"I smelled so polluted after opening night, my own mother almost passed out when she hugged me," he said.

"Story of my life," I said. "That's just me, normal day."

"Not like this," he boasted. "I smelled like a condemned barn."

"You probably just smelled like milk," I said. "You always smell like milk."

"I do?" he asked.

So, that happened.

I told him he smells like milk. Ugh.

"Yeah," I said.

"Thanks, I guess?"

"Should we check on Lightning again?" I asked, because could we please call the podiatrist to yank this huge foot of mine off my tonsils? *You always smell like milk*—really? I mean, he does. But *really?*

"Okay," Emmett said. "Maybe if we get there early enough, we can convince my wrangler to show you around backstage."

"Your what?"

"Wrangler," he said. "The adult in charge of me at the opera."

"She wrangles you?"

"Yup," he said, and winked. I laughed. He is such a nut. "Alicia. She's really cool. You'd like it backstage, I think, all the costumes and wigs and dressing rooms and horses and secret passageways."

"Horses and secret passageways?"

"Yeah," he said. "It's pretty amazing there. I'm gonna miss it a little. This is probably my last opera." He smiled, but it wasn't his normal full-face happy smile. His eyes were sad.

"Why?"

"Growing, a little. Finally. Starting to. Anyway, it's time. It's all little kids there, which is, whatever, what it is. Plus my voice is changing."

"It is?"

"Thanks, yes. It is. You can only hear it when I sing, which I don't in this opera—just stand around. You know, acting. I'm a super."

"Are ya now?" I kidded him, trying to get his eyes back to happy. "Super, huh?"

"That's what they call it if you don't sing."

"To make you feel better?"

"Maybe. Anyway, so this could be my last chance to show you the cool stuff. Like, as an early birthday present."

"Oh." I don't know why that made a lump form in my throat. It took until he was pitching the idea to my mom before I could speak.

Obviously Mom said no. I knew she would.

My parents are so overprotective. And then I can't even be a normal kid and throw a fit, because their eyes are always scanning my face, making sure I am happy, happy, happy. I am the wind beneath her wings, Mom used to sing to me at bedtime. So if I storm out like, *I hate you*, they'd crash to the ground and then what?

My cousin Hadley told me last Thanksgiving that on their way to Grandma's, her mom was saying that after Bret died, she really thought my parents might both kill themselves or just die of broken hearts, but then I was born and I basically saved their lives. Especially because I was such a bundle of joy. Such a fat, giggly baby. She was wondering if I was still so sweet, now that I'm in eighth grade.

"Am I?" I asked Hadley.

"Eh," she said. "You were really cute when you were little, and then you got funny-looking, and now you're kind of starting to even out."

"Oh, um, thanks?" I said.

"No offense," she said.

"None taken," I lied. That's when I started saying, "None taken," even when people didn't say, "No offense," to me. I think that's hilarious, but it hasn't become a thing, so maybe I should stop saying it.

"Bret was beautiful," Hadley had said, shrugging. "That's what everyone used to say about her: 'What a beautiful little angel.' Then they'd say, 'Thank goodness for Gracie, such a bundle of joy.'"

So I was like, "Wait, so my job is to be a bundle of joy all the time, my entire life?"

Hadley said, "Basically, yeah. Well, that, and to not die."

So when my mom said no this afternoon, that I couldn't walk down to Lincoln Center with Emmett tonight to drop him off at the opera, I only argued for half a minute and then I shrugged and said, "Sorry, Emmett."

He said, "No worries," and we went back to my room.

"It's fine," he said. "Just an idea. Some other time. You okay?"

"I'm always okay."

"Uh," he said. "Yeah? Show your work."

"What?"

"Always? Who's always okay?"

"I am," I said. "Haven't you noticed?"

"No, sorry."

"None taken," I said. So much for stopping that.

"You sure?" He tilted his head a bit. "Maybe a little taken?"

"Totally," I said. "None taken ever! Show me that video before you have to go."

"Okay," he said, giving me some serious side eye. "If you—"

"I wanna see it!" I said, maybe more enthusiastically than he'd anticipated, because he leaned back like I was a hurricane blowing in.

"Wow. Okay." He pulled his computer out of his bag and showed me the video of AJ falling asleep while eating leftover pad Thai. It was hilarious and, horribly, adorable. My phone buzzed, like, a billion times, and so did Emmett's, but we were like, *No.*

"I'm putting mine on airplane mode," Emmett said. "Enough."

"Seriously." I switched mine off too, without reading the infinity texts clogging up the screen.

"You guys hungry?" Mom called.

Emmett and I shrugged at each other and trudged down the hall with his computer. Mom placed Bret's handprint plate on the counter in front of us, loaded up with Milanos and sliced strawberries. "Do you want popcorn?" Mom asked. "I make excellent popcorn."

"The best," Emmett said, mid-Milano. "But I should probably go down and eat a quick dinner and take a shower before opera, because, hashtag sweaty guys."

"Hashtag sweaty guys!" I said back.

We fist-bumped.

"Let's never call ourselves that again," I said.

"Yeah, no, never," Emmett agreed.

"It's like you two have your own language," Mom said.

"I should . . ." Emmett tilted his head left.

"Yeah." I followed him up our hall toward the front door.

"Bye, Emmett!" Mom called after us. "Have a good show tonight!"

"Thanks," he said, stomping into his sneakers without bothering with the laces.

"Yeah, good luck," I said at the door. "Or do they say, 'Break a leg,' in opera?"

"They actually say either *toi toi toi* or *in bocca al lupo*."

"Sorry, huh?"

"I don't know what *toi toi toi* means, but the other one means: 'into the mouth of the wolf.'"

"Gross."

"Yeah, but cool also. Like, 'Go on into the mouth of the wolf, you!' So you say that, and then I say back, *Crepi il lupo*, which means, 'Die, wolf!'"

"Okay."

"It's a weird world, there."

"You sure that's opera world and not fairy-tale world?"

"Definitely want the wolf to die there, too."

"And don't take the shortcut," I added.

"The shortcut?"

"In a fairy tale," I said. "You never wanna take the shortcut through the forest."

"Excellent advice. The shortcut is always the wrong move."

"If you find yourself in a fairy tale, at least."

"And a forest." Emmett leaned against the door next door and accidentally rang the bell. "Oops!"

"Oh no," I said. "Better run for it!"

"Never. Gonna. Happen," Emmett said.

We smiled. Nobody lives in that apartment. An old guy whose mother used to live there before she died keeps his stuff in there as if it's his storage closet, because it's rent-controlled so why not? Emmett and I always used to imagine, what if we could break in and make it our secret clubhouse? My mom once saw the guy whose mother's apartment it was, as he was leaving. She asked if he'd sublet part of it to her, let her use maybe one room as a writing space. "Never. Gonna. Happen," he growled at her, and bobbled away. Since then my family and Emmett's all call him the Never Gonna Happen Man.

We almost never see him. So we weren't actually worried,

just kidding. But then the door to the apartment opened, and the red-faced, walrus-mustache man growled at us. "What's the big idea?" He pushed out into the hall, past Emmett, to loom over me.

"Sorry," I said. "No big ideas here, promise."

Emmett leaned against his open door. "How's it going, sir?" he asked politely.

"Don't ring my doorbell!" the man barked. He lurched back into the apartment, past Emmett, and grabbed a lumpy gray sack. Then he came back out, yanked the door closed behind him, bopping Emmett out of the way, and harrumphed his way past us to the elevator, where he stood, grunting and shifting his weight with annoyance, without looking back.

"Never," I whispered to Emmett, who immediately started laughing.

"Gonna," he whispered.

The elevator dinged. Never Gonna Happen Man muttered, "Troublemakers," and then stomped into the elevator. As the door slid closed behind him, Emmett and I both whispered, "Happen." And doubled over laughing.

"Okay, so," I said to Emmett after we were able to deal again. "Well, then, um, toys, toys, toys, and, you know, go kick the wolf in the teeth, you."

"Thanks. Kill the wolf, you."

"Frickin' wolf," I said.

"Hey, speaking of never gonna happen . . ." Emmett started.

I was already saying, "See you tomorrow." So I asked, "Wait, what?"

"Nothing, tell you later. You're good?"

"Totally fine, yeah," I said. "Tell me what later?"

He grinned, shrugged, and then dashed away, down the stairs.

22

PROBABLY WON'T SNOW, SO

Turns out, while I was busy learning multiple ways to say good luck in opera-talk, AJ had asked Sienna what she was doing tomorrow before my party.

After lots of analysis and unanswered texts just to me (**GRACIE, where are you? you have to help me, help, help, help**, for example) Sienna had decided to text back to AJ that she had tennis in the morning and then was just hanging out with me until my party.

He texted back: **cool cool**.

What do you say to **cool cool**? Was that flirting or dismissive? Had she said too much or left it too open or what? Was **tennis in the morning and then just hanging out** the stupidest, most buzz-killiest response in the history of responses?

there have probably been stupider responses in history somewhere, I texted her. **I mean odds are . . .**

Sienna texted, **GRACIE! where have you been? help, help, no disappearing!!!**

Riley texted us both right then in a group chat, asking what the latest was, and apologizing because she'd been busy learning to wing-tip her eyeliner from her sister. So Sienna had to retell the whole saga. But just when Sienna got to the **cool cool** part, Riley texted us: **Sorry, GTG—heading over to a little thing at Beth's . . . <3<3**

wow, okay, Sienna texted just me.

We didn't care that she was going to a Loud Crowd thing we weren't invited to, even though all the girls in that group were invited to my party the next day. Whatever. Not too awkward. Ugh. I should've just made plans with Sienna and my parents like last year. We went away to Washington, DC, for the weekend and saw all the sights. It was great. But Mom suggested maybe this year I'd like to do something with a bunch of friends, and I guess I didn't want her to think I was a loser who had none. I don't even like a lot of the people I invited.

SIENNA: do I talk too much?

me: no! absolutely not. Riley is just rude. On purpose

Riley texted only Sienna to say Michaela and Beth and Fern and Fara and she all thought maybe Sienna should put on a bikini and take a selfie in it, because, #boys, and also, then she could say something about how it's supposed to be hot out tomorrow.

Sienna copied it to me and was like, **no way, never, not doing that, omfg, no.**

me: hahahaha

SIENNA: sorry, but really, why did you tell those people anything? I'm not mad. well, maybe a little, but srsly, Gracie. ☹

I sat with that for a second or two and then I decided too bad—I owed Riley nothing. So I texted Sienna back.

me: I actually didn't. okay here's how I found out that AJ likes you: Riley asked me to find out who AJ likes because she likes him! and it turned out AJ didn't like Riley. he likes you. so point for AJ for taste. the second after I told Riley that AJ liked you, not her, she puked at Dorin. so that's what all that was about

Sienna didn't respond for a while. I regretted everything.

why didn't you tell me that? she eventually texted.

It took me a bunch of tries to not insult myself and my stupidity, but after a lot of feeding the delete button, I ended up with the sad truth of: **she asked me not to tell you**.

Nothing. Nothing. I flopped down onto my bed and counted backward from one hundred, and if I got to zero before Sienna responded, I would drop out of school and just go sit at the Hungarian with a book and a croissant for the rest of my life.

I got to eighty-two before Sienna texted back: **you're a good person, Gracie.**

can't respond w/o insulting myself, I texted back, though I was flooded with relief. Literally flooded. Sweat stains on my pillow.

Riley wants me to send bikini selfies to them so they can help me choose, Sienna texted. **I'd rather stick a fork in my eye**.

We decided she should text a cross-eyed selfie back to Riley and be done with that conversation because wow, weird, no.

For AJ, we settled on the selfie idea (they are the experts, so), but one with her wearing her hat and mittens and captioned with: **unless it snows tomorrow.**

Sienna thought maybe that sounded too random, but I convinced her that random is funny. Also, it gives him an opening to say, *No, it's supposed to be hot*, since it is, and then maybe he could say something like, speaking of hot . . .

Sienna texted back, **oh no, don't even.**

Michaela and Beth and Riley all think it's an awesome idea, I texted.

She texted a picture of herself looking, I'm not sure—mad or stunned or both. But still so cute.

hahaha, jk, I texted back, followed by a bunch of emoji hearts. Not sending selfies to duel hers, thanks anyway.

She sent back a bunch of hearts and some tortoise emojis too.

Then she went to find her mittens and hat.

Mom said, "Hey, let's go to Thai Market, Gracie! What do you think? You love Thai Market!"

I do, so I said, "Okay, be ready in five minutes?"

That's what happens when she says no to something I want to do, like walk down Broadway with Emmett just now. She comes up with something wonderful, like go out to dinner at a restaurant I like. She fully doesn't need to do that. I could just be disappointed or sad or annoyed for a minute and get over it. But no.

"Or we could go somewhere else if you want," Mom said, outside my door. "Are you more in the mood for sushi?"

"No," I said. "Thai Market is great. Just, I just need a few—"

"Five minutes," Dad said. "But then let's go because I'm hungry and I have work I have to do after."

"Okay," I said. "Almost ready—I'm just . . . watching something on YouTube." I don't know why I lied. I could have said I was texting with my friends. We have the unlimited texting plan. It's not that. I just . . . I don't know. Felt like lying.

"Can't you watch YouTube later?" Dad asked.

"Yeah, but I'm almost done," I said, actually watching nothing, just waiting for a picture of Sienna in a hat and mittens even though it's mid-April.

adorable, I said honestly when it came through. **absolutely perfect**.

So Sienna texted AJ the hat and mittens and *unless it snows* pic.

"Let's go," Mom said, still outside my door. She knocked and then opened it without waiting for me to respond. "You ready?"

"I . . ."

Sienna texted me a stressed emoji and: **he's not responding.**

he's thinking, I reassured her.

"No phones, please," Dad said, peeking in my door. "Let's just have a civilized dinner and talk with one another."

"Hold on," I said. "I just . . ."

I looked at my buzzing phone. A line of **????** from Sienna.

"I just have to—"

"No, you really don't," Dad said.

"Hon," Mom said to Dad, her hand on his arm. "Just give her a minute."

what happened? I texted Sienna.

AJ had texted her a screenshot of tomorrow's weather report, high of seventy-nine, low of sixty-two, 35 percent chance of rain. And then, one second later, a picture of himself looking adorable and confused with the caption: **Snow?**

"I just have to text Sienna one quick thing," I told my parents.

"I'll push the button," Dad said, heading toward the elevator.

"Okay, cool."

Sienna was busy Snapchatting me her crazy variety of frowny faces, but I was like, **no that is so awesome. that was a good answer.**

What I didn't text was: I wish someone had texted *Snow?* to me.

Or maybe that he had sent me that exact picture but then texted something like, *Hey, but if it snows, let's go sledding.* That would be such an awesome response. Oh, I'd be even more in love with a boy who texted, *Hey, but if it does snow, let's go sledding,* to me after a weather report showing highs near eighty degrees, and a picture of himself looking all confused and adorable and so much like, well, AJ.

Hahahaha. Never. Gonna. Happen.

No boy is ever going to text me flirty things if I am such a control freak that I would want to edit his texts and make them funnier, more random, more agreeable. Well, not that that's the only reason no boy is ever going to flirt with me by text, but . . .

Nope. Shut that down.

Anyway, do I even really want a boy to flirt with me? The pressure! And really, what would be the payoff? Just, like, knowing somebody likes you? That would be nice, I guess, but maybe not worth the side effects? Maybe going out with somebody would be awesome and romantic like Michaela and David, but then you eventually have to kiss, which is a whole thing in itself and possibly disgusting. And then, after that, if the Loud Crowd is a guide (and they are, in all things except academics, social activism, and selfie selection), after a few times of kissing you have to fight and then break up (unless you are Michaela and David), which seems like a lot of work and drama to end up back where you started.

I don't know. Maybe I'm immature.

Sour grapes?

The thing is, Sienna is the most chill, even-tempered, anything-is-fine, social-justice-conscious person I know, and just trying to flirt with a boy—who has already said he likes her so she is at absolute zero risk of making a fool of herself—is completely freaking her out. She's as off-balance as I was when I got an ear infection the summer before sixth grade and couldn't turn to the side without wobbling, or swim for a week.

Maybe she needs a Z-Pak. Antibiotics actually are a good invention.

"Gracie!" Dad called from inside the elevator. "It's here. Let's go!"

So I texted Sienna that I was going out to dinner with my parents/no phones, so good luck and I'd catch up later, but for now she probably shouldn't go swimming.

I knew that would confuse her a little, but she's used to me, and anyway, it was worth it, because I got into the elevator all smiley, which, with my parents, is wonderfully contagious.

23

HBD2M

12:01.

It's officially my birthday. Fourteen.

I'm twice as old as my older sister ever got to be.

There are so few Hallmark cards for celebrations like that.

So. Maybe I'll go get myself a glass of water. Or take Lightning out to play, even though, like my parents, she's sleeping. I could give her a string bean, despite the fact she already had one this week. Still, #yolo. I'll only turn fourteen once. Some people never get to.

Okay, that actually was fun. That crazy tortoise chased after the string bean in such a sprint, she was belly-flopping across the kitchen floor, her mouth wide open. I love that someone, even a tortoise, can end up as discoordinatingly psyched as I get about food.

We sat in the almost dark of the kitchen together, my tortoise and I. Only the light of the bathroom from the apartment across the air shaft lit up the room, and even that was just really a dim streak highlighting our stand mixer and making a stripe of light across the hardwood floor. I had to laugh, because we were some hella party. The happy little tort chomped at her string bean and I chomped at my chocolate chips. (I know I said a glass of water, but I lied. It is my birthday; leave me alone.)

"You and me, pal," I said to my tortoise. "We are the Awkward Club."

She smiled up at me.

Not even kidding. I know I am delusional, probably, but I swear she did smile. Luckily I had my phone with me, so I quickly snapped her picture. So cute. I was thinking, I should text somebody that most adorable ever picture, but all the parents are like, *Cell phone curfews. No texting after ten p.m.* Which usually I am fine with, because I love sleep, but: smiling tortoise!

She walked away and snuggled into the corner of the kitchen under the cabinet. Oh, Lightning, you are my role model. You get tired? Off you go to sleep. You have enough of being with people? Good-bye. If only.

On my way back up the hall to my room, a new text lit up my phone. It was from Emmett, who I realized must be on his way home from performing at the Met:

HBD2U.

Oh, Emmett, you best person ever.

As I was holding the phone, about to text him the picture of Lightning smiling, in came a Snapchat with a picture of him in the back of a taxi, looking hugely exhausted, his hair all messed up and standing up in points, stage makeup smudged under his eyes, and the caption **Totally fine, yeah** under it.

He really is the best.

How horrible is it that one tiny terrible part of me was thinking, *Wouldn't it be awesome if it was AJ who did all that for me?*

Because I completely suck.

Obviously it is way past the time for me to get over any of those weird blasts of complete potentially belly-flopping discoordination every time I think of him. Enough.

I mean, I know AJ likes me. We're pals. He just doesn't *like me* like me; he *likes* likes my best friend. Which is awesome. AJ and Sienna make a great couple. I am completely happy for them.

I checked my Facebook. Emmett had posted a message on my wall that just said **first** at 12:01.

He's so great.

The Emmett stuff is just friend stuff, and please, let's not start overanalyzing that! I am not the romance type of girl. Why would I even imagine myself in, like, a romantic entanglement thing, with AJ or anybody?

With Emmett?

Who really is the best? And has the cutest face of anyone, all crinkly eyed and seeing the humor and the deeper meanings?

Nope. Stop it. Stop it. Nope, nope, nope. He's just being a good friend, a buddy, funny. Not being romantic. If AJ did those things for Sienna, sent her *HBD2U* one minute after it turned to her birthday, obviously, he would be flirting.

Context is everything, according to Ms. Valerian, our English teacher, who is so smart, she went to Columbia twice, including grad school. Context: Emmett is pretty much my best friend other than Sienna, if you think about it. It doesn't need to be contaminated with romantic nonsense. Me and Emmett?

No.

He doesn't *like me* like me, obviously! Emmett has so much going on, he probably doesn't have time to even think about stuff like liking somebody, and if he did, he'd probably like somebody little and cute like he is.

Not lurchy and big-nosed like me.

We're buddies. We're solid. We have epic battles of video-game boxing and board-game Stratego and racing each other up and down the stairs in our building, and a couple of times we tried playing chess. We are the best partners for school projects.

We get each other's jokes. We have infinity inside jokes.

Stop.

Anyway, Emmett is like me: not the romantic type. We've

got bigger fish to fry in this world, really. Emmett and I both fully get that.

So: relax. No need to go concocting fantasies about me and AJ, me and Emmett, me and any boy. That's nothing. Nothing to see here, folks; move along, move along. The romantic story does not and will never star *me*, the big, doofy, funny sidekick. Which is fine, more than fine; it's awesome. I'm the second, in every sense. And who doesn't like seconds? Hahahaha. Everybody likes seconds. Especially me.

Poor Emmett just wanted to say happy birthday. Chill.

I swear I used to be a sane person, when I was thirteen. Things could happen without me flipping out all over the place like a dying bluefish on a dock.

And besides, he is shorter than I am, so as everybody (now including me) apparently knows: Never. Gonna. Happen.

24

SURE

My original idea was a picnic at Turtle Pond just with Sienna and Emmett, but Mom and Dad thought that might be kind of nothing. So instead, I invited fourteen random people and we went down to the ferry. It seemed like such an awesome idea when I was planning it with Mom—the Statue of Liberty! Ellis Island! Two subway lines! Three ferries! Like a class trip!

It didn't work out as well as I had hoped.

Maybe fourteen is too old for something like the Statue of Liberty and Ellis Island to be fun without permission slips. Everybody smiled quickly when I looked in their direction. The more polite kids even pretended to be interested in reading every single explanation as Dad insisted we all needed to do. Ultimately it was just hard on the feet, all that standing around.

And getting rained on was super fun. So much for the 35 percent chance.

While we slumped in the depressing interior underbelly of the ferry heaving damply back toward Manhattan, Dorin sat next to me and whispered, "Thanks for inviting me."

"I'm really glad you could come," I said. I considered lying to add I was so sorry I got her e-mail wrong or something which was why she didn't get the original invitation, but I decided to stick with just letting it be the awkward thing it was.

I had asked Mom at Thai Market the night before if I should just invite Dorin last minute. She said it would be fine with her and Dad to add another friend. Over tao-hoo todd and soup, we discussed the pros and cons of how I could invite her, and what excuses I could make for why she was being asked so late. We decided maybe it would end up more awkward than it was worth, so better to just leave her uninvited.

But then the pad see-ew came and I was still feeling bad about it, so we decided, better to be awkward and nice than awkward and excluding. Not that everybody in the grade was invited, just fourteen kids (plus me) out of fifty-four, but somebody like Ricky Wu wouldn't care, and Dorin clearly did. So I texted her, right from the Thai Market table:

me: hey a few of us are going to the Statue of Liberty and Ellis Island for my bday tomorrow. can you come? meet at my apartment at noon? I'd really like it if you could . . .

I hit send and then we moved on to: Should we get the little foam Statue of Liberty headbands for everybody as a sort of loot bag souvenir thing, even though they are crazy-overpriced and also silly? Dad didn't think the boys would want to wear foam headbands, but I said, "Are you kidding? They so would."

"Okay," he said. "What do I know? Kids these days."

Before our sticky rice with mango showed up for dessert, Dorin texted back.

DORIN: Sure! That would be great! I'm not sure if I'll have time to buy you a present before then, but maybe there's a tortoise thing downstairs in the store I could give you.

I texted back not to worry about a present and that I was happy she could come, which I actually sort of was. I hadn't thought about it before, but in truth I like Dorin a lot more than most of the people I'd intentionally invited.

"I'm glad I came too," Dorin said, beside me in the ferry underbelly. "It's a really fun party."

I had to laugh a little. That was such a lie. The rest of us, including my parents, all looked like we were being transported to prison. Despite the Statue of Liberty headbands on most of the heads. Every boy's head, I noted.

"No," Dorin said. "I mean, it's sort of fun, other than the rain and the boringness! For my half brother's party, he just turned five? We had a piñata and it was so adorable? He did the cutest thing with . . ." And on and on. I smiled and nodded, but I couldn't honestly make myself listen to the details of her half brother's adorableness again.

When I was five, I had a piñata too. A duck piñata. Something made me cry that morning. Okay, it was that I wasn't allowed to eat my entire cake all by myself before the guests arrived. As I wept about that injustice, my nana told me, "If you cry on your birthday, it will rain on your wedding day."

The randomness of that idea stopped me from crying, because: what? Why would I care if it rained on my wedding day? I was *five.* I didn't even care about, like, later that afternoon. But also, whether I cried or didn't one day when I was five years old would affect weather patterns years in the future? Was I a *superhero*? I controlled *future rain* with my *emotions*?

I had learned a song about the rain cycle at Hollingworth Preschool that year, and it hadn't mentioned anything about me. Did other people know about my superpower?

When the adults got distracted by the first guest ringing the buzzer, I smashed my face down into the cake. I really wanted the whole thing for myself, and that was my plan. It wasn't a *good* plan, I realized, while my face was still three layers deep.

So I waited there, head inside the cake, thinking maybe this would stop happening. I was scared that I would be in serious trouble as soon as I looked up.

But eventually I needed to breathe, so up I straightened. I saw Mom laughing instead of yelling. I was so confused. She thought it was hilarious. She was too busy taking pictures of me (blinking, waiting with tight knees to get hollered at, frosting coating my eyelashes like fairy-goo mascara) to even consider punishing me.

Since then, I haven't cried on my birthday (or really ever), even today in the belly of the ferry, with all my friends sitting on benches silent and glum, and Dorin chattering my ear off. Successfully avoiding wedding-day storms!

In case I eventually get married. Some people don't, obviously. And realistically, what's my shot at walking down the aisle in a poofy white dress if nobody ever texts me things like:

AJ: Hey, so, you wanna be like going out? With me? It's fine if you don't.

Which is what AJ texted Sienna, from Emmett's apartment where he and Emmett and the other boys were changing out of their wet clothes into some of Emmett's dry ones before coming back up to my apartment for pizza and cake.

Sienna held out the phone for me to see what he'd written.

"Wow," I whispered to Sienna. Silently I vowed, despite everything, *not* to face-plant into my cake this time.

The girls who had come back to my apartment all gathered

around to see what had happened. We covered our mouths and held in screeches and hopped around like my floor had turned into burning coals.

"Everything okay?" Mom called from down the hall.

We stopped, hands over mouths, frozen like the gargoyles on the building up the street, our eyes all bugged out.

"Yup!" I yelled. "Fine!"

"What do I say?" Sienna whispered.

"Do you want to?" I asked her.

"I guess so," she said.

"So, say 'I guess so,'" I suggested.

"No!" Riley said. "Gracie! She can't just . . . *I guess so*? Do you have a concussion?"

I had to laugh. "A concussion?"

"What should I say?" Sienna's eyebrows were so scrunched, her forehead looked like a traffic jam. "You guys!"

"Say okay," Beth suggested. "Casual. This is so exciting! Ben asked me out last night, so now there will be all these couples for graduation parties!"

"If any of you last," Riley said. "Just saying: graduation is still a full month away."

"Way to be positive," Beth said poutily.

"Or say yes," I told Sienna. "Yes is good."

"Not too formal?" Sienna asked.

I shrugged. As if I were some kind of authority on how to respond when a boy asks you out. Too bad Michaela had to leave early. She and David were going to a concert with her grandparents.

"Yes is fine," Beth said.

"Or maybe ask if he has a concussion," I suggested. "That's hilarious."

"Gracie!" Ilaria shrieked. I was surprised, because Ilaria rarely speaks at all. I always forget she and Jo exist outside of math class. They were sitting together on my bed. How random that I even invited them.

"Everything okay?" Mom asked again. "I'm making popcorn!"

"Awesome!" I called back.

Sienna unlocked her phone to reread the ask, and then looked pleadingly at me.

"Say yes," I whispered. "It's okay for it to be a little formal. It's a big deal."

"Or maybe just say okay," Dorin suggested. "Okay is a good compromise."

Riley rolled her eyes, as she had at every syllable Dorin had uttered all day.

"Okay is good," I said. "Okay is perfect."

"One plain, one pepperoni, one mushroom and olive?" Dad yelled down the hall.

"Great!" I answered. "And garlic knots!"

Sienna closed her eyes and took a deep breath, her phone cradled in her hands.

"Of course! Double order!" Dad yelled back.

When Sienna opened her eyes, I whispered to her, "Or how about: *Sure.* That's more confident but also less formal, you know? Like, *sure.*"

Riley nodded. The other girls nodded. We had a treaty. Hallelujah.

Sienna typed: **sure.** "Should I add any kind of emoji or anything?"

"Nah," I said. "I think simple is better."

"That's true," Jo said from the bed. Still there. "For most things."

"Okay," Sienna said.

"Hit send," I said. I could hear the popping start in the pot on the stove—one, two, waiting for the third to pop . . . There it went. Mom was pouring in the rest of the cupful of kernels and then adding some butter, which was sizzling on top. The lid clanked on. Mom really does make the best popcorn. We had two minutes until she'd call us to come eat it.

"Are the boys on their way up?" Mom asked.

We all grinned at one another. "I guess!" I yelled. "Soon!"

Sienna was holding her phone, staring at her *sure* text in its little rectangle, until the screen went black and she had to unlock it again.

"Hit send," Beth whispered. "And you'll be going out with AJ!"

"You do it," Sienna said, thrusting the phone at me.

"Me?"

"It's your birthday," she said.

"So?"

"And that way we're, like, more in it together," she said.

Leave it to Sienna, who is the most awesome, to include

me instead of taking the spotlight for herself in this most romantic moment of her life.

I put my hands on top and slowly lowered my thumb toward send. "You sure?" I checked, hovering a millimeter above it.

Sienna's eyes met mine, and she smiled, all calm now. "Sure," she said.

So I hit send, and just like that, Sienna and AJ were going out.

25

SO MUCH BUZZ, HOW DID MY PARENTS NOT NOTICE?

Ten minutes later Emmett and AJ and the few other boys who hadn't bailed already came back upstairs. It was a huge commotion. Luckily the pizza came fast, and it was all a big blur of everybody grabbing slices and chomping away. Well, not Riley, because, she told us, a slice of plain pizza has 285 calories—also, fun fact, a bagel has between 245 and 500 calories. She hasn't eaten a single bagel since she was ten, which the rest of us all thought was tragic. "How do you live in New York City and not eat a bagel in four years?" Emmett asked her. "How is that not grounds for eviction?"

"I think it might be," I agreed.

"You have to run five miles to burn off one dry bagel," Riley said. "Just saying."

The calorie announcement didn't slow most of us down, pizza-wise, though probably some of us would have had at least one or two more slices if she hadn't said that about how many calories. It's like when they list the calories in Starbucks—maybe you end up getting the salted caramel cake pop for 180 calories instead of the cranberry orange scone for 420. You still get something. Stamp out world hunger, starting with my grumbling belly, but the calorie count, man. Sucks all the fun out of things.

Then Mom brought out the cake, which was so pretty. Everybody sang "Happy Birthday." I blew out the candles. I did not face-plant. I managed to wish for a long happy healthy life for myself and everybody I love instead of *Please let cake have zero calories* or even *Make him like me instead.*

Those of us unafraid of (or just fully over) calories because, *birthday cake*, enjoyed the nice big slices Dad cut and served us. People handed me their bags and boxes and gift-card envelopes as they put their shoes on and said good-bye. Most of us are allowed to just go home independently, even though it was almost eight p.m.

"Phew," Dad said, gathering up pizza boxes, paper plates, and plastic cups to bring down to the basement.

"Yeah," Mom said, yanking the trash bag out of the bin and replacing it immediately with a fresh one. "I'll come down with you."

Then the only ones left in my apartment were me and Sienna, and Emmett and AJ, who was sleeping over at Emmett's. The four of us alone together never would have been awkward before, but now, well. We couldn't talk. We looked at Lightning sleeping in her bin for a minute, and then I decided to open my presents, as an activity. Sienna's was a whole stack of stuff, so I started with that. There was a book about taking care of Russian tortoises and a copy of *Cyrano de Bergerac*, which we saw with my parents at the Vivian Beaumont over February break and we both said we should read afterward but we didn't, and also a toddler toy of a stuffed tortoise that lights up and shines little stars on the ceiling for an hour while you fall asleep. In the card taped on top were two certificates from her parents, one a one-hundred-dollar donation in my name to firstbook.org, and the other, one hundred dollars to turtleconservancy.org.

Wow, I love her whole family *so much*.

But I tried not to go on and on about it, because obviously that would make Emmett and AJ feel bad. I didn't want to open their gifts right after that, so I opened the one, beautifully wrapped, from Riley, Michaela, and Beth. It was a set of three bracelets from Somebody and Somebody. (What are their names? I think they both start with *A*, but I have to make sure before I send the thank-you note.) I had to origami my hand to squeeze it in. Still, they are very pretty once on. I didn't feel too much like one of Cinderella's ugly stepsisters in front of my three discouragingly slim friends, there, trying to smoosh into a too-small shoe, getting those bracelets on, no worries.

Dorin's gift was a log. Well, half a log, hollowed out.

"Okay," Emmett said. "Sort of random, but cool—who wouldn't want half a log?"

"It's for Lightning," I said.

"Ah," he said. "Well, I'm sure she'd share."

"Maybe I could use it when she's napping," I agreed. "When I'm feeling loggy."

Sienna and AJ were smiling tensely, not talking.

Emmett's gift, in a big multicolored bag full of yellow tissue paper, was a hat. It had a wide brim, a big red feather, and a nylon see-through top.

"From the guy we love on the corner?"

"Who else?" Emmett said.

"So perfect," I said, showing it off to everybody. "Is this the most hilarious hat you've ever seen? I love it!"

"You guys are so weird," Sienna said.

"I think it's the best hat he had," Emmett said. "But there was also a lime-green fedora, so . . ."

"No, this is the clear winner. The air-cooled top? This *feather*? Come on." I plopped it right onto my head and let everybody, including Mom and Dad, who were up from the basement, snap pictures of me.

AJ gave me a twenty-dollar gift card to Starbucks. Which is totally great. It is. Forget what I always say about *I will never give a gift card as a present because it's completely impersonal and just sad.* I'll definitely be happy, buying treats there for myself. And maybe for friends! Who even knows! I slipped it into my wallet.

"I wasn't sure what to get you," he said sadly. It was adorable.

"This is awesome," I said. "Seriously. And just my size! See how well it fits?"

He was blushing. Yikes. I had to look away.

We decided to watch *The Incredibles* because, why not, and nobody had any opinions or preferences. Sienna and I flopped down onto the couch. Emmett and AJ sprawled on the floor. Mom and Dad watched with us for a few minutes, sitting in chairs, but then went to their room.

I don't think AJ and Sienna said one word to each other or even made eye contact, including when we said good-bye and the boys went down the stairs to Emmett's, but still, obviously something major had changed. There was so much static electricity in the room as we watched the movie, I'm surprised the TV didn't conk out and the birthday balloons hovering over my leftover cake on the table didn't attach themselves to our heads.

26

THE MORNING AFTER

By the time I wandered down the hall from my bedroom the next morning, Lightning was already munching away at her plateful of salad. Mom and Dad were watching the Sunday political argument shows, which they call the talkies, on TV. Dad's hair was damp from his post-run shower, and bagels still warm from Absolute were covered with the Shakespeare tea towel in the big blue bowl on the counter. I peeked underneath it. Yes. A salt bagel was plunked right on top.

Dad smiled when I said thanks.

"Happy birthday, sweetheart," he said. "What a horse's patoot!"

"Me?"

"What?"

"I'm a horse's patoot?"

"No," Dad said, his eyes dragging away from the TV. "This—ugh. Are you listening to this bankrupt excuse for a boneheaded foreign policy?"

"Trying to," Mom said.

"Trying not to," I said.

"Where are my glasses?" Dad said, his favorite question. They were beside the bagel bowl, so I brought them to him. He only wears them for movies and the talkies. But he can never find them. Sometimes he's already wearing them.

A diabetes medication commercial came on as Sienna wandered down the hall in what she always wears when she sleeps over: my softest too-huge-for-her purple flannel pajama pants and so-old-it's-practically-silk, inherited-from-Mom Springsteen concert T-shirt. "Talkies?" she asked.

Mom was pouring boiling water from the kettle into the teapot. "They're in rare form today," she answered. "Gonna need a *lot* of tea."

Sienna laughed. She's used to my parents and how enthusiastically angry they get at most of the talkers on the talkies. It's the only time anybody ever sees my parents mad—in front of the talkies, Sunday mornings. I sampled a cucumber slice from the plate loaded up with freshly arrayed cukes, red onions, tomatoes, lemon wedges, and a small pile of capers (eww, but Sienna and my dad like them) on the side. We're good at Sunday, my family; Sienna always says so.

"Are the boys coming up for brunch?" Mom asked me.

"Oh," I said, scoring a slice of Havarti from the cheese plate. "I don't know. Maybe?"

"There's plenty if they want to come," Mom said. "Daddy got whitefish *and* salmon *and* Tofutti *and* scallion cream cheese."

"I couldn't remember which you said Sienna likes!" Dad protested.

"I like anything," Sienna said.

"See?" Dad said. "I love this girl! She likes everything! So that's what I bought!"

Mom laughed. "She didn't say *everything*! She said—"

"I could text Emmett to see if they're coming up," I said. "Or . . ." I turned to whisper to Sienna. "Or you could text AJ."

"Oh," she said quietly. "Nah."

"You sure?"

Sienna held out her phone in her palm like she was her eighty-seven-year-old great-grandmother, Abuela, unsure how such a thing might work, afraid it might explode like a grenade in her hand if she did it wrong.

"What?" I asked.

"You do it," she whispered. "I can't. You text him and pretend you're me again."

"It's on," Dad said.

"Seriously," I said.

"Hmm?" Mom asked me as she went over to sit next to Dad on the couch, carrying fresh mugs of milky tea for each of them, both psyched, their glasses on, ready to get happily furious at the people arguing about incomprehensible world events.

"Nothing." I took Sienna's phone and pressed my thumb onto it, since we have each other's thumb prints set to unlock our phones. I went to the texts and scrolled through all last night's texts from "Sienna" to AJ and from him back to "her." Well, from him to *us*, but he didn't know that. It started about ten minutes after AJ and Emmett went downstairs after *The Incredibles*, just twelve hours earlier.

Sienna and I both smiled, rereading them. *Wow*, I thought. *We went on and on, didn't we?*

In person AJ is a little shy. I used to think he was definitely nice but a little boring (except for his eating style). Turns out by text he's way funnier, and more random. We had gotten into a weirdly natural and hilarious rhythm, me and AJ. We had texted back and forth for over an hour, even after Sienna started losing interest. She started watching a *Planet Earth* episode about lakes on my computer, and falling asleep. But AJ didn't know that. He doesn't and can never know it was actually me he was flirting with, while he was picturing my adorable though sleepy best friend.

I read all the way through our long text conversation, right through to the end where, after a few minutes when I thought maybe he'd fallen asleep, AJ texted: **you asleep?**

me (on Sienna's phone, answering honestly sort of if I was supposed to be her): yeah

AJ: Drat. I can't fall asleep. I'm already thinking about what to eat for breakfast. I'm hungry all the time lately.

me (still as Sienna): me too! my favorite kinds of lakes:

1. great

2. cornf

AJ: Hahahaha. 3. Frostedf

"What does that even mean?" Sienna asked, reading her texts and AJ's.

"Frosted F-lakes?"

"Yeah, but . . ."

I shrugged and smiled, trying to stop myself from wishing those texts could live on my phone instead of Sienna's, and not only so I could reread and enjoy them over again whenever I wanted. Also, honestly? So AJ would know it was actually me he was going back and forth with. Connecting. So it could be legit between him and me instead of . . .

No.

Shut up, shut up, shut up.

"His sense of humor is so like yours," Sienna said.

"That must be why you like him," I said. *Stop sweating.*

"Maybe he asked the wrong girl out," she said.

"No!" I said. *Inhale. Exhale.* "You guys are such a good couple."

"Do you actually think so?"

"Yes!" I said, trying to believe myself. "You are both so nice. And sporty. And adorable. And smart. And sweet. And oh, Sienna. Just trust me."

"I do," she said.

"I know," I admitted. **who wants bagels?** I texted from Sienna's phone to AJ's, and handed it back to her.

"That's good," Sienna said. "Phew." She followed me to the bathroom. "Simple."

While we were putting our hair up, AJ texted back: **Who doesn't want bagels?**

She showed me. I smiled. "Cool. We should hurry, I guess."

"Answer," she said, trying to pass me the phone.

"You answer!"

She grunted and stared at the screen. "Fine. Fine. I can do this."

"You so can."

She chewed on her lower lip, thinking. "Should I just say, *Come on up then*?" she asked. "Or something funny?"

"Like what?" I asked, loading up both toothbrushes.

Instead of answering, Sienna put down the phone beside the sink and started flossing, inches from the mirror.

I started brushing. Flossing is So Much.

"Maybe we could say something to him about, like, people who don't want bagels are just wrong?" Sienna suggested, talking around the floss. "Or, like, maybe . . ." She sat down, dejected, almost deflated, on the edge of the bathtub. The piece of floss dangled from between her teeth like a sad walrus whisker. "I don't know, Gracie! I am normally a functional person. You do it. You're so much better at this than I am!"

"No, I'm not," I assured her. "You're just panicking. What were you thinking?"

"Promise if it's dumb you won't let me send it?"

"Promise," I said through my toothpaste. "What?"

"I don't know." She got up and went back to flossing while she talked. "I was thinking maybe we could say something like, *Well, gluten-intolerant people don't want bagels!*"

"Hmmm." I spit out my toothpaste and then rinsed out my mouth, to delay. "That's a little insensitive to the gluten-intolerant, don't you think?" I said. "My cousin is gluten-intolerant, you know."

"Oh! I'm so sorry," Sienna said, her voice and face instantly flooded with anxiety. "I didn't know! Which cousin? Shane? I didn't mean . . ."

"Just kidding," I said. "Sienna. Chill."

"Oh," Sienna said. Her high cheekbones had bright-pink blotches in the centers. She tossed the floss and started brushing really aggressively. "I have lost all sense of humor or, like, sense."

"All sense of sense," I said, nodding. "That's excellent."

Sienna shook her head and kept brushing. No wonder her teeth are so shiny; she takes really good care of them.

To cheer her up and calm her down, I put my hand on my hip and rolled my eyes, imitating Riley, and said, in Riley's breathy not-that-I-care-but voice, "I got a callback for a print ad for gluten-free bread last month."

Sienna laughed so hard, she choked on her toothpaste. "Ow, ow, that's terrible!"

I flipped my hair the way Riley does. "So many auditions."

"I'm a model!" Sienna imitated, still brushing.

"Commercials," I said. "Print work. I'm dating Pierre, who is also a model, like me, because, well, I'm a model. Bow down, losers."

"Ugh, she's the worst." Sienna stopped brushing for a sec when a glob of toothpaste fell onto her phone. "Tell me what to do." She stood there, her mouth erupting with toothpaste foam, looking like she'd gotten rabies.

"Well," I said. "Okay, first? My advice? Spit."

"Huh?" Bubbles of toothpaste foam floated from her mouth into the air between us.

"Spit?" I repeated.

She did, and waited.

"Sienna! Okay, now just text back anything, nothing—something like, *We have Absolute up here, so if you want some, you better hurry.*"

"Okay, I am literally just typing exactly what you said," Sienna said, splashing water into her mouth and onto her face. She is the messiest tooth-brusher. I put her phone into the towel rack's cubbyhole, next to a box of Band-Aids, so it wouldn't get wet.

"What did you say again?" she asked, drying partially off.

"Sienna," I said. "You got this."

"Ugh," Sienna grabbed her phone and followed me to my room, saying out loud while she typed, "We have Absolute up here, so if you want some, you better hurry."

By the time she sent it, I was changing into clothes. Nobody sees me without a bra on. No *baboom*, *baboom*, thanks.

"I can't even," Sienna said, flopping down onto my bed. "My clothes from yesterday are still damp and all I have for today are more tennis clothes and oh, Gracie . . ."

I told her truthfully that she looked fine in my pajamas, and she should absolutely stay like that.

"You sure?" she asked.

"You look adorable," I said. "I swear on Lightning's life."

"You are everything," she said to me.

"I really am," I agreed. "An everything bagel."

"What would I do without you?"

"Miss me," I said. I turned around to see if she thought I looked okay, in my new shorts and the dug-out-of-the-messy-pile-of-presents T-shirt Ilaria and Jo had given me as a birthday gift.

"That's great on you. You're completely awesome. I, on the other hand—"

"Don't," I said. "Remember our pact."

"I, on the other hand," she insisted, "am so sick of myself, I'm starving."

"It's hungry work, flirting," I assured her.

"Well, then I think I am going to have to eat all the bagels."

"Bagels have between 245 and 500 calories each," I said in my best Riley voice.

"Good," Sienna said. "I need all the calories in the universe." She regathered her hair into a messy half ponytail/half bun, not even checking how it looked before we went down the hall. I did the same to mine. Hers looked cute. Hopefully mine did too.

27

IN A SANE WORLD, I COULD NEVER HAVE A CRUSH ON A BOY WHO LIKES BLUEBERRY BAGELS

By the time Dad got up to slice bagels during the next talkies commercial, the boys were ringing our doorbell. AJ was wearing Emmett's pajama bottoms, which were three inches too short for him, but his hair was neatly combed. Emmett was wearing shorts and a T-shirt, but his hair was a minor mountain range, tilting west.

"Nice hair," I said to Emmett, to keep from saying anything about how adorable AJ looked in those pajama bottoms. Look away, look away.

"You like that?" Emmett said. "Took an hour."

"Totally worth it," I said.

Meanwhile, everybody else was crowded around the center island, where the bagels and toppings were all arranged.

Mom lifted the Shakespeare tea towel off, and Dad asked what kind of bagel everybody wanted. He doesn't trust anybody to slice bagels except himself.

"Are there any blueberry?" AJ asked.

Silence.

"Um," Dad said. "No." He didn't say sorry or what's your second choice because . . . blueberry?

"Dude," Emmett said, putting his hand on AJ's arm. "No."

"What?"

"Blueberry?" Emmett asked.

"Blueberry bagels are the best!" AJ said.

My parents and Emmett and I all had to take a sec. Sienna just kept her eyes down, a small smile on her pretty mouth.

"Never say that again," Emmett said to AJ. "I love you, man, but you actually can never say that again."

"Blueberry bagel?"

Dad clutched his chest. Mom covered her face with her hands. Sienna was laughing her bubbly adorable laugh by then.

"Even in the same sentence," Emmett said.

"Even in the same paragraph," Mom said.

"In fact," I said, pointing at the bowl of berries near Sienna's arm. "Those blueberries? They're pushing it."

"Throw those out immediately," Dad agreed.

"I love blueberries," Sienna said, chivalrously, in AJ's defense.

"Everybody loves blueberries," Emmett said. "Just keep them out of the . . . Can I have an everything, please?"

"Yes," Dad said, and started slicing him one. "Good man. And you? Tall boy? Pull yourself together. An everything? Garlic? The salt is for Gracie."

"An everything, please," AJ said humbly. "How does everything not include—"

"Stop," Emmett warned him.

"Never mind," AJ said.

We ate almost all the bagels and all the toppings Dad had gotten, too. So, score one for him, overbuying at the bagel shop, *not.* And score another one for AJ, who, though barely saying another word beyond thank you to my parents, now that he'd been schooled on what is fine and what is unspeakable, bagel-wise, managed to eat four bagels in the time it took the rest of us to eat one.

Lightning chased me around until I added some extra radicchio to her special plate, the one we got free with some soap from L'Occitane last year and used to just keep unused in the cabinet. Emmett cleared his plate all the way into the dishwasher and then sat back down next to me on the floor to watch Lightning eat. He and Daphne were really young when they got their rabbit. Before Fluff, he had a goldfish named Fishy.

He and I had a moment of silence for the tragedy of stupid pet names given by children too young to know better.

My parents shut off the TV after the talkies finished. Emmett and I were trash-talking about whether a tortoise could really beat a rabbit in a race. I was trying to focus only on the tortoise and the hare, hahahaha. Don't look up at the counter again even though AJ eating is one of my favorite things to watch.

"Anybody want more?" Mom asked.

"Just a few mangled sample bagels left," Dad said, holding the bowl toward the ill-fitting-pajama-pants wearers sitting at the counter. They both shook their pretty heads politely.

I could have eaten a second bagel, but I held back. I'd only had the one, plus okay, like, one tiny bite of an everything and one slightly less tiny bite of an egg, but those were the sample bagels. And those bites were just for taste. Just-for-taste bites of sample bagels have—fun fact!—between zero and screw you calories.

28

BUT WAIT, THERE'S MORE

Late that night my phone buzzed while I was lying in bed, watching the stars from the toddler turtle toy dance on my ceiling.

EMMETT: Hey, are you asleep?

me: yeah you?

EMMETT: Yeah.

me: oh sorry

EMMETT: ☺ You didn't throw away the boxes and bags and stuff yet, did you?

me: what stuff?

EMMETT: BD gift wrapping stuff.

me: still a mess in here don't judge me

EMMETT: Your present from me wasn't just the awesome hat from the guy on the corner. There's something else in that bag.

me: uh-oh if there's a puppy in there it might be dead bc it's v quiet here now

EMMETT: Oh no, poor puppy, oh no, oh no, I should've mentioned it before, oh no.

I got out of bed and dug through the bag from Emmett, stuffed with yellow tissue paper and, lo and behold, yeah, no puppy, but there was a small paper sack in there. I opened it. A necklace with a small chunk of yellow something, maybe a rock, dangling from it, held on by some silver wire.

It was very cool looking. I'd seen it on the Guy at the Corner's table this past week and thought it looked like something Future Me would wear. But I hadn't said anything out loud to anyone. Just pictured it, around my neck, when I was older.

And hey, now here I was, older. Fourteen.

Not old like that Future Me lady at Hungarian, reading a novel and eating a croissant-comma, but still, on my way toward becoming her. Was she wearing a necklace like this? Is that why I noticed her, or why I noticed the necklace?

I put it on and latched it behind my neck, under my mess of hair.

I took a selfie, even though I was all ragged from a long-haul weekend of turning fourteen. Still, I told myself, it was just Emmett. So I sent the picture to him, with **thanks** scribbled under it.

EMMETT: Perfect.

I sent him another selfie of me making a goofball fake-model pose, like I was Riley modeling this necklace.

EMMETT: I'd buy it.

me: ☺ you already did bozo

EMMETT: You like it? The guy said I could switch it for a supercoolio visor if you don't.

me: no way. this rock thing on a chain is worth more than every visor in the world put together

EMMETT: Do you know how many visors you'd have to stack to get from the top of our building to the moon?

me: no

EMMETT: Phew.

me: yeah cuz that would be a weird piece of knowledge to have

EMMETT: Even tho u r 14 now.

me: yeah so I know stuff now watch out

EMMETT: Yikes. Okay, good night.

me: good night

me: hey Emmett?

EMMETT: Yeah?

me: I really like it thanks

EMMETT: Good, I'm glad. It looks nice on you.

me: •••

I kept starting words and deleting them. I had no idea how to respond to **It looks nice on you**. The typing and deleting went on under my fake dancing stars for approximately a billion hours until I fell asleep, holding my phone, still wearing the necklace.

29

A RARE BEAUTY

I was really into making bead necklaces when I was in nursery school, and I loved wearing them and giving them as gifts. In fact, Emmett and I got to be friends at Hollingworth Preschool when I used to make him bead necklaces and he wore them all the time. He never came to school or, the moms say, left the apartment without wearing one of my creations. We don't remember any of this, but we believe the moms, because in every single picture of Emmett ages three and four, he has a bead necklace on. According to the stories our moms tell, I always gave him my best necklaces (unclear how I determined the rank, but I was supposedly very definite about the quality) and kept the second bests for myself. In my second year at Hollingworth, though, I made my best ever bead necklace, the Platonic Ideal of Bead Necklaces. They knew this because that was the one and only bead necklace I couldn't part with, couldn't even give it to Emmett. I asked Mom and Dad over and over, "Isn't this one the most beautiful?" And they, being them, said that yes, wow, that is a rare beauty of a bead necklace.

That's what they called it: a rare beauty of a bead necklace, and after a while just Rare Beauty. That one I kept for myself, and stopped wearing any of my others. I gave all those second- and third-rankers away to grandparents and lesser nursery school friends, who I'm sure were thrilled to receive my rejected bead necklaces.

I wore Rare Beauty every single day when I was in the big-kid afternoon class at Hollingworth, and through the following summer. Until one day on the subway platform at Seventy-Ninth Street, waiting for the uptown 1 train, I got mad at Mom for some nothing; Mom can't remember what it even was. Probably I was just hungry or tired so I wanted her to make the day start over from dawn *and she didn't.* I was so massively little-kid angry, I took Rare Beauty off and threw it down on the platform near Mom's feet.

Mom said, "Gracie, please pick up your bead necklace. Come on, sweetheart."

And I said, "No! You pick it up!"

Mom says she wishes she had just picked it the heck up. But it was hot, August in the city, and it had been a long day, and I sounded bratty and she didn't like that tone of voice, so she said, "No, Gracie. I'm not picking it up. You threw your bead necklace on the ground. You need to pick it up. The train is coming, sweetheart. Please pick up Rare Beauty."

"You do it," I said. "You pick it up."

I turned my back on my necklace, and her.

Mom said, "I'm not picking it up, Gracie. If you don't pick it up right now, Rare Beauty will be lost forever."

I crossed my arms over my chest and refused to look at it. The train came. We got on without my necklace. And obviously Mom was right; it was lost forever. It's not like I can go to the MTA lost and found now and say, *Hey, ten years ago I left a rare beauty of a bead necklace on the uptown platform of the 1 train at Seventy-Ninth Street. Do you have it?*

Oh, certainly, miss! Here it is in this special box. We've been wondering when somebody would come to claim it because, wow, it sure is a rare beauty!

Don't think so.

So that was the end of that perfect bead necklace. Mom says I didn't make myself a new one and never mentioned it again, so she didn't either, until I was, like, ten and didn't remember the incident at all. She was laughing, telling it, but then she got sad at the end. She said she has always regretted that she didn't just grab it at the last second and shove it into her pocketbook, so at least she would have it as a memento.

"It's okay, Mom," I said last time it came up, this past fall. "I don't even remember it, except in the story, and anyway, it was completely my fault. You totally made the right call."

"But you were just a little child," Mom said. She blinked twice and went to take a shower. That was weird. It was just a bead necklace. How much of a rare beauty could it even have been?

This morning I woke up with a jolt. I was in the middle of a dream where Mom was telling that old story of the time I threw down Rare Beauty, and she stopped where she always stops, but this time not because she got suddenly sad but instead to go get the secret small blue box of stationery and photos of Bret out of her sock drawer. In it were no old photographs. Instead the blue box held only the most perfect bead necklace anyone had ever made. As she put it over my head, Mom said, "I picked it up at the last minute. All this time, I was just saving it to give back to you at the right moment."

My hand was clutching the necklace Emmett had given me.

30

WHAT I LEARNED TODAY AT SCHOOL

1. Nothing.

31

WHY

All everybody wanted to talk about was Sienna and AJ: what a cute couple they are, how he had asked her out by cute texts, and when are they going to kiss? Maybe at the party at Michaela's house? Which is on Wednesday after the volleyball and baseball games and isn't actually a party. It's just chilling (we don't say *hanging out* anymore; keep up). All the guys on the baseball team and the girls on volleyball, chilling at Michaela's.

Sienna is sure it would be fine for me to come too, and in fact, she's not going unless I go too, so I absolutely have to go.

Even though Sienna is on the volleyball team, she doesn't usually hang out with (I mean chill with) the Loud Crowd after. Usually she just hangs out with, well, me.

I finally got used to not saying *have a playdate with*.

The only really good thing that happened all day was that in English, we found out our next book is *Brown Girl Dreaming*, by Jacqueline Woodson, and raise your hand if you already read it (if I had seven hands, I couldn't raise them enough to be accurate about how many times I read that book last summer; so good), and Emmett raised his hand too. We were the only ones. So the two of us have to take a quick quiz on it tomorrow, and if we both pass, we will be in a group of our own.

I guess we'll probably read and discuss a different book chosen by Ms. Valerian. Or, more likely, we will discuss Sienna and AJ, because truly that is all there is now.

I really hope the alternate book is good so I don't regret admitting that I already read *Brown Girl Dreaming.* I could have just shut up and reread it, and been partners with Sienna if there's a project. That would've left Emmett alone in the alternate book group though, so maybe it's good I got excited and raised my hand without thinking.

It's definitely a good thing I don't need to reread *Brown Girl Dreaming* tonight to prep for tomorrow's quiz because I am very, very busy making up funny, subtle, not-too-romantic but not-too-stiff responses to the texts AJ is sending to Sienna.

It's crazy easy to respond to him. It's like he sets me up for what to say, and I set him up right back, and then he zings it back to me, just perfect for me to respond.

But I don't respond to him. I respond to Sienna. Who copies and pastes.

And tells me how amazing and awesome I am.

Wouldn't it be so much more efficient if AJ and I just texted directly? (This is the thing I did not text to Sienna. Instead I texted: **aww shucks**.)

Also I am very busy watching Lightning sunbathe in a patch of light near the living room window-doors, while I try with every brain cell to invent a reason I can't go to a party with all the kids who are on teams, including the entire Loud Crowd, at which Sienna might get her first kiss. Even though I just texted my best friend that obvi I will come if she wants me to, and Sienna responded: **omg, yes, I need you there**.

Even though if the situation were reversed, I know she would just be psyched for me, and I would need her there for support, and she would be there, no question.

32

LUCKILY WE HAVE THE UNLIMITED TEXTING PLAN BECAUSE

AJ: So r u going 2 Michaela's Wednesday?

SIENNA (via me): Not sure—are you going?

AJ: Yeah probably

SIENNA: (didn't respond because she was still texting with me to figure out what to say when he popped up again)

AJ: You should def come. It'll be fun. Michaela's parents usually order in lots of food and we eat up on the roof.

SIENNA (me): the roof? yikes.

(Sienna has been to Michaela's; we all have. She knew what that meant, that they'd eat in the party area on the roof garden of Michaela's building. It was a way of stalling on our part, and also of teeing up something for him to say back, is what I told Sienna. She was doubtful, but she trusted me. She always trusts me.)

AJ: Hahahaha there's a whole party area up there, chairs, tables, lights

SIENNA (me): oh cool, much less sketchy than it sounded. ;-)

AJ: Yeah a party on a different kind of roof would be kind of overwhelming.

SIENNA (me): or underwhelming.

AJ: When ideally you really want a party to just be whelming.

SIENNA (me): the perfect amount of whelm is such a tough thing to achieve.

AJ: Right? If it's either over or underwhelming we're so leaving

SIENNA (me): we demand exact amounts of whelm!

AJ: whelm us properly, world!

SIENNA (me): what do we want? to be whelmed! when do we want it?

AJ: Always!

SIENNA (me): exactly. including now, but: gtg, ten pm . . . parents . . .

AJ: May take me a while to fall asleep.

SIENNA (me): same.

AJ: GN. Stay whelmed.

(**Sienna to me:** GN?)

(**Me to Sienna:** good night?)

(**Sienna to me:** oh, obv. ugh, can you get a concussion from flirting by text? will you just take my phone and deal from now on?)

(**Me to Sienna:** hahahaha. just say you too. GN)

SIENNA (me): you too. GN.

me: that was awesome Sienna. are you so happy?

SIENNA (actually Sienna, texting only me): yeah. I am. kind of. also, exhausted? but that was fun.

me: ya think? that was completely wonderful

SIENNA: what will happen though if we have to talk face to face and you're not there to help? he's gonna think I turned into such a dud.

me: no way. you're funny and sweet and perfect. and you're so pretty he'll forget how to form words anyway so it won't matter.

SIENNA: oh then we'll be the perfect couple, going like duh and ummm and staring at our shoes.

me: maybe that's why people end up kissing

SIENNA: because they have nothing to say to each other?

me: good a reason as any

SIENNA: let's meet early tomorrow morning, so I never have to face anybody without you, okay?

me: sure sounds good. xoxoxox

SIENNA: hahahaha.

33

THE LATEST

Guess I left my computer open on my floor while I slept last night. I woke up to find Lightning, sitting on it, looking up at me, very pleased with the status update she had just posted for me.

It was:

iiiiiiiiiiiiiiiiiiiiiiiiiiiiiiwwwwwww222222222222222222w wwwwwwwwwwwwwwwwwwwwwwwwwwwww , ... kkkkkkkkkkkkkkkkkkkkkkkkkkkkk kfffffff6666666666666668

It's better than any I've posted lately, so I figured I'd leave it.

In case I was feeling all kinds of creative and genius for writing other people's messages for them: *so can my tortoise.*

34

ALONE TOGETHER

On the way to English today, Dorin asked if I wanted to come to the pet shop on Wednesday. "Since Sienna's going to that party," she said. "I thought you'd be free."

"Oh," I said, wondering how she even knew that. "Thanks! But I can't. I have to . . . I told my mom I would do a . . . a thing, help her."

"Oh," Dorin said, smiling. "Okay. Maybe some other time."

"Definitely," I said. "Thanks. That would be fun, hanging at the, you know."

"Yeah," she said. "I love your necklace. That's new, right?"

"Yeah," I said, touching it. "Thanks. Birthday present."

"From your parents?"

I was just going to lie and say yes, since I was in a lying groove already, but that seemed weird, a lie for no reason, so I said, "No, Emmett got it for me."

"Wow," she said. "That's . . ."

"That's what?" I asked.

"That's really romantic," she said.

"No, not at all," I explained. "It's just . . ."

Riley lunged forward and yanked Dorin close enough to whisper to her. I couldn't hear what Riley asked.

"Emmett," Dorin said to Riley, her voice definitely loud enough. "Why?"

Riley shhh'd Dorin, raised her eyebrows twice, then smiled at me.

"What?" I asked her.

She chuckled to herself and then turned to whisper something to Beth, whose eyes flicked up at me and then quickly away. Ms. Valerian told me to sit down at the table in the back. When Emmett showed up, she sent him to the back table too and then handed us facedown quizzes on *Brown Girl Dreaming*. She explained that assuming we both passed the quiz—"Don't worry; I know you both will," she said, winking—we could work alone together on the extra project, since we didn't have to do the nightly reading of twenty pages and then answering five questions about it. I had thought we'd get assigned some cool other book, but this was even better.

We flipped over our papers when Ms. Valerian said to, and quickly filled in the answers. It was an easy quiz, just confirming that we'd read the book, no big deal. Except that everybody kept glancing over at us. Every time I looked up, heads whipped away.

As if it meant something about us, that we were segregated at the back table, both taking a quiz on a book, just the two of us plus my necklace, which, why did I wear it to school, two days in a row? Or, worse, that I *thought* it meant something about us, about Emmett and me, as if I wanted it to be, well, more.

Come on. Obviously not. It was just Emmett and me, forced to take a quiz and then work on a project together. We just both happened to have read a particular book already. Plus, we're friends. We do stuff together all the time, always have.

I would never want to mess that up, or take a chance of messing that up.

We're friends. No subtext.

It's just Gracie and Emmett, you guys. Not, like, Michaela and David, or Sienna and AJ or Beth and Ben or something. Yikes. Look away, look away. It's just two not-super-popular, kind-of-brainy regular kids, discussing quietly whether it would be more fun to make a diorama or a triptych poster board or do a short scene with reading aloud some portions of *Brown Girl Dreaming* or if that's not culturally okay because I am a white girl and he is an only somewhat brown boy, being half-Filipino and half-Israeli. But still, we could both relate to so many of Jacqueline Woodson's poems—and even with the ones we didn't directly relate to, we felt like, *Yeah*—so maybe reading them in some kind of organized or dramatic way, or memorizing them and presenting them to the class, would be okay, or even good?

It was cool, working on that, fun and almost relaxing, just doing schoolwork for a change—until I accidentally glanced up again and saw so many eyes flicking away from us. I groaned so Emmett would know I wasn't thinking anything other than what a bunch of deluded losers they all were, to think this was anything. He did the same, and then we looked back down at our books. His book was in much nicer shape than mine. It looked practically new. I should be less brutal, gentler with my books, I decided. And then, hallelujah, it was time to go to Spanish, so we made a plan to get together later and work on the project more after he got home from opera class.

Anyway, that felt like the big drama of the day, until I got home from school. Well, that and the continued plotting about how and whether the Sienna-AJ kiss would happen Wednesday on the roof of Michaela's building: Would they go off alone behind the storage shed? Or go down to Michaela's to get more food and kiss in her kitchen? Or just be holding hands and accidentally start kissing in front of everybody, like Michaela and David sometimes do but they've been going out for months and also have both kissed other people before so they know what they're doing and are unlikely to faint or miss like Sienna fears she might?

I walked home alone in the bright sunshine of the afternoon, since Sienna and the rest of them had practice for all their sporty things, and Emmett had left school a little early for an opera rehearsal (so I guess that's what he meant by after he got home from opera—not class but rehearsal). I walked home, thinking about that, about how you can think you know a thing, but then it turns out you're wrong—usually just little things, like if a person has opera class or rehearsal, or, like, if a person (a different person from the one in the opera example) definitely wants to kiss your best friend, or maybe in fact he's scared too, or unsure if he really likes exactly her in a kissing way. If it can turn out that your assumptions are sometimes just flat wrong, doesn't that make even the hard concrete of truth feel alarmingly spongy beneath a person?

I said hi to the homeless woman outside the bank and assured her that, yes, I was keeping up my studies, and said hi to the jewelry/hat guy on the corner, but I didn't point out my necklace to him. I wasn't wearing the hilarious hat, which would have been more noticeable. I just said hello and he smiled with his mouth but not with his sad, sleepy eyes. Some people have sad eyes even when they're smiling. The rest of the way down the block toward home I wondered what might have happened to the jewelry/hat guy in his past to make his eyes so sad all the time, and also thought about the fact that there's very little likelihood I'd ever find out.

You can't just go up to people and say, *Why do you seem so sad?* as if you were asking, *How much does that amazing hat cost?* You just have to wait and wonder.

Usually.

35

ALONE

I'm not a baby. I'm fourteen. I've been in my apartment alone before. I have my own keys. I come home to nobody plenty. It's not that.

I walked in, hung my keys on the hook, and said hello. Nobody answered. The ceiling fans were off and the AC hadn't been turned on in any of the rooms, but the windows were all closed, so it was hot and still in the apartment. All the lights were off. No note. I had the feeling, maybe the fear, that they were gone, both of my parents—that they had left and not taken me with them, maybe had moved back to Boston or just gone away together to Tahiti or Europe and forgotten all about me. It was just for a second, part of a second, that old worry I used to have in nightmares and, well, daymares. Before I could even fully feel it, I knew that was ridiculous. Never. Gonna. Happen.

They would never move on without me. Right?

And then I remembered what day it was.

The day Bret died.

April 17. Eighteen years ago today, my sister died, and I had gone through the whole day selfishly not remembering. Not even realizing in the morning that my parents were unusually quiet, folding their lips into their mouths, trying to smile more than actually smiling when they looked at me. Not even really looking at me, now that I thought about it. Most of the time they scan my face, checking for any sign of sadness or worry, watching me, looking too closely until I want to scream at them to leave me alone. But this morning they weren't really looking at me at all. They were trying not to cry in front of me, maybe, or just, like, thinking. Having stuff in their heads that had nothing to do with me, that was prior to me.

Once, when I was little, Dad was telling some story about when he was a kid and went to a football game with his grandfather. The point of the story was his grandfather's Boston accent, but I interrupted Dad to ask if I had gone to the game with him and his Boston grandfather. He said, "No, sweetheart. I was a kid. You weren't alive then!"

I remember that freaked me out. I remember asking him, "Wait, I was dead? When was I dead? Why didn't you ever tell me I was dead before?"

"You weren't dead," Dad said, laughing. "You just weren't alive yet. I was a little boy."

He gathered me up onto his lap. But I wasn't in the mood to be cuddled. I remember his cheek was scratchy against mine, and I pulled away to look him in his blue eyes. I wanted to get to the bottom of this, because it seemed like I had just stumbled upon some secret truth about myself that had been kept from me. "If I wasn't alive, I was dead! Right?"

"No," he said, rubbing his head the way he always does when he's thinking, and smiled at me, his bright little girl, so interesting, so sunshiney. "You weren't dead; you just *weren't* yet."

"I weren't what?"

His eyes crinkled appreciatively. "You weren't born yet. You weren't anything."

"Was I with Bret?"

He blinked, and the joyful crinkles dissolved instantly and the whites of his eyes turned red before tears formed in their inside corners. I remember watching it happen, the tear in one of his blue eyes gathering itself into a small globe. I watched to see if it would fall. It didn't.

"No," he whispered.

"Was I ever with Bret?"

He shook his head, and the tear shook loose and got caught in his bottom lashes.

That's all I remember of that. I don't know what happened next, or where Mom was during it. But it's not a story they've told me; it's my own memory. What I wish I had asked him then, or ever, though, is: How did you move on from that? How do you and Mom not just cry all day every day? How do you sometimes laugh, find things funny, buy bagels, care about politics or stupid little kid bead necklaces or anything at all, when your child died?

And: If I died, would it finish you off? Or would you move on from that, too?

Either answer is horrible.

Is why I've never asked.

And why I sometimes, like this afternoon, have a horrible panic that they will someday forget about me and just move on.

In the silence of my overheated apartment, waiting for them to please come home, I Googled their names and Bret's and today's date but eighteen years ago, and I read about my sister getting hit by a car in a town just west of Boston when she ran out into the street. The driver, who stopped immediately after, was taken to the hospital too, despite not being injured in the accident. Bret's funeral was three days later. In lieu of flowers, it was requested that donations be made in Bret's name to the charity of your choice.

I knew all that, basically. I knew it already. It's my family history.

One news story said Bret died in her (my) mother's arms at the hospital before they could do anything to save her. That was a bit I hadn't known. *In her arms.* There were more details I also didn't know in a few other articles. I kept reading and then clicking away. Then clicking on one more link, feeling guilty and nauseated, like somehow I was going through my parents' private stuff and if they caught me, I'd be in trouble.

At Emmett's once, when we were little, we were playing in his mom's closet until his sister came into the room and shouted at us to get out! Respect people's privacy; what was wrong with us? We shrugged at each other, not knowing what or if something was wrong with us. The dresses were silky, was all, and pretty colors, and we were walking through them, pretending our faces were cars at a car wash.

I kept clicking, despite Daphne's question pounding in my head: *What is wrong with you?* One short article a few months after the accident said the lawsuit against the driver of the car was being dropped. I clicked away. Lawsuit? First I heard of it. I cleared my cache. Not that my parents would check my browsing history (or know how to) or be mad if I was looking stuff up about Bret and what had happened. Probably. Still.

I closed my computer and sat on my bed and cried.

I wasn't crying for my parents' heartbreak, or for my sister who didn't get to live long enough to have a best friend or to help her best friend get a first boyfriend or first kiss, or to get either of those nice things for herself.

Honestly? I cried for myself, for being alone in my apartment while my parents were out together somewhere I wasn't included in, having forgotten to even leave me a note saying when they'd be home because they were busy remembering their first daughter, the beautiful one, the one I was supposed to but will never replace.

36

OOPS

We ordered in sushi. I took a deep breath before mentioning her name.

"I was thinking about Bret today," I said.

They stopped eating. Dad had a piece of tamago suspended midway between his plate and his open mouth. Mom let her chopsticks clink onto her plate, and rested her hands in her lap. "Yeah," she said. "Us too."

"Did she like sushi?" I asked, which was not at all what I wanted to say.

They each smiled a tiny frown-smile. "She was kind of a picky eater," Mom said.

"She mostly liked pasta," Dad said. "With butter."

"And rice," Mom said. "White rice."

"And berries," Dad added. "At least that was something not white."

"I wish I had known her," I said quickly.

Mom took a deep breath and then another. "I wish you had too."

"Do you think, though . . ." I started, but couldn't finish. My throat was stopped up.

"Gracie?" Mom asked. "Do we think what?"

"You probably wouldn't have had me if she'd lived," I blurted. "So I guess I should be grateful in a way that she died! Hahaha!"

They both stared at me.

I burst into tears. And ran to my room.

So that went super well.

My whole idea, while they were out and I was home alone, was to cheer them up when they got back. That is, after all, my job in life. Right? As Riley pointed out in her otherwise ridiculous insult-fest, Bret's death wasn't my tragedy, really; it was my parents', and Bret's. I *weren't*, then, when she got hit by that car and died before she even got treated at the hospital, died in my mother's arms.

And I wasn't there before that, when she was alive. Even now, it's not my place to be sad about the death of some random seven-year-old I never met. I may have spent an embarrassingly large amount of time imagining conversations and a relationship with Bret, but imagination is just playing. It's for children. I'm fourteen now. Twice what Bret ever was.

Grow the heck up, I growled at myself. *You are not a child anymore.*

That just made me cry more: *Not a child anymore.*

I grabbed my pillow to stifle the sound as I sobbed for a good minute more.

Pull yourself together, I told myself. *Seriously. You're actually just not a child, despite your childish tears; that is simply a fact. You're not in mourning, because you're not part of the family that was Bret's. You never even met her.* I forced myself to breathe slowly, in for ten, out for ten. Fourteen years old and teaching myself how to breathe. My parents must be so proud.

According to what I read on the Internet after I cleared my cache again but before they got home, carrying takeout sushi: a good way to help someone who is grieving is just to ask gently in an open-ended way about the dead person's life—without pushing, just be available to hear about the grieving person's memories.

But instead of helping them to talk about good times they had with Bret, I had turned instantly into a drama queen Looney Tunes baby, ruining dinner. And then asking for a few minutes to myself, please, when Mom knocked on my door, instead of apologizing like I knew I should.

"Okay, sweetheart," Mom said, outside my door. "I just hate it when you're sad."

"I know," I said.

"Okay," she said, sounding hopeful but a little unsure. "Do you need anything?"

"I'll scoop out some ice cream," called Dad from down

the hall. "We got you some cookie dough! And cookies from Insomnia! The deluxe one you love!"

"Thanks!" I yelled back. "Be there in a sec."

I listened to Mom's footsteps quietly padding away. I cried for a few more minutes, but really, the urge had passed. I felt kind of self-indulgent at that point. Dangerously close to the selfish turd Riley had accused me of being. So I pulled my hair up and myself together. Time to go apologize, because, really.

My parents deserve a little sunshine.

37

GONNA BE SO FULLY PREPARED FOR HIGH SCHOOL, WITH ALL THIS LEARNING I'M DOING

Sienna was already at school when I got there this morning. She smiled as soon as she saw me. "What happened last night?" she asked.

"What do you mean?" Had I butt-texted her a video of the disaster I'd caused in my family?

"You didn't respond at all!"

"Oh," I said. "I . . . My phone . . . I turned it off and didn't—"

"Gracie!"

"I'm sorry." We walked up to the eighth-grade hall together. "Why? What happened?"

"No," Sienna said on the way up the stairs. "I'm sorry.

Who even cares, right? I mean, when you didn't answer, I just didn't text anything to AJ. I got my homework all done by eight. It was relaxing, actually. I played multiple rounds of Apples to Apples with the monsters before they went to bed."

"Sounds nice," I said.

"What's wrong?"

"Nothing," I said. "It sounds nice!"

"I'm so sorry," she said. "I didn't mean—"

"No!" I smiled. "I know. Sienna. It's fine."

"You sure?" She scrunched her little nose. "How's Lightning?"

"Awesome. Did I tell you Emmett calls her Tempus?"

"Why?"

"You know, like, 'Time flies'? *Tempus fugit?* Because she's so fast."

"Okay."

"Or sometimes Flash. Once he called her Bite Size."

"Don't let him pet-sit."

"Seriously." I took out my phone to show her Lightning's most recent pictures but then slipped it quickly into my pocket when I heard shoes with heels approaching. No phones in school. If a teacher catches you with a phone out, she's supposed to take it away.

"Definitely didn't see that," said Ms. Valerian, striding past us.

"Thanks," I said to her back.

Sienna and I smiled at each other.

"She's great," Sienna said. "And you're right: *Brown Girl Dreaming* is so good."

"Right? Emmett and I might read some of the poems out loud for our project."

"That's a great idea," she said. "So, okay. Last thing I'm saying at all about the party or AJ or any of that?"

"Don't worry about it," I said. "What?"

"You're coming to the game later and then Michaela's, right? Please?"

"The thing is, my mom really—"

"Gracie," Sienna begged. "You don't have to come to the game, boring, but—"

"How could I not go to Michaela's?" I smiled again. "Would I miss your first kiss?"

She practically tackled me, shushing me so much.

38

PLEASE LET THIS NOT HAVE HAPPENED

It was an accident.

And now it's a secret.

But I don't know for how long, because now it happened and there's nothing I can do to fix it or make it not have happened. I hate myself.

I can't breathe. I have to pull myself together and clean up the mess before Mom gets back home and sees the shattered plate in three chunks and a hundred slivers and infinity molecules of powder on the kitchen floor.

I just . . . I don't know. We always put cookies on Bret's handprint plate. That's where cookies go. Well, not always. Sometimes. Usually not when we're bringing them to somebody's house. Why didn't I just put them in a Tupperware?

Why is there no delete key in time?

Why can't I just turn time back? Not years. I'm not even asking for that. Just two minutes' worth of rewind—tocktick, like on the DVR, like the time-warp trumpeter—and I would leave the plate with Bret's handprint on it up where it belongs, in the cabinet above the fridge.

But no.

Tempus just ceaselessly *fugits*. Ticktock, always: ticktock. Never ever tocktick.

Mom was about to come home to walk me down to the party at Michaela's, where my best friend was probably going to have to kiss her new boyfriend, maybe in front of everybody, and I had said I would bring homemade cookies. I figured it would give me something to do, and keep me from having to watch them all sportsing after school.

I stood there in my kitchen, staring at the mess all over the floor and on my socks, hating myself. *Think, think, think.* Lightning was heading toward me, looking like she wanted to taste some plate dust. No!

I got the broom and dustpan to collect the mess that used to be the plate that had had my sister's handprint on it. Swept it all up and then dumped it into the garbage pail, like just trash instead of the most precious piece of art my family ever owned.

Gone. The plate Bret had indelibly touched. *Fugit.*

How many times have I measured my hand against Bret's handprint? My whole life. That funny, precarious *R*, the ridgy brushstrokes. Her handprint.

The powdery bits were drizzling down among the garbage in the bag, sounding like the rain stick I used to love shaking. It had sounded so peaceful. This didn't. Not the good kind of pretend rain.

I grabbed the bag out of the bin. I had maybe five minutes, possibly less. Tying the bag as I dashed down the hall, I looked for my shoes. Forget it. I grabbed my keys.

I hate going down to the basement; it creeps me out. Dad usually brings down the trash, even though that's kind of gendered behavior. Mom told him not to make me go down myself when he asked me to bring it one time. Maybe it's dangerous down there? She didn't specify why. I just assumed it was too dangerous for me alone. What if there's a bad guy? How would I escape? Who would hear me scream?

I had myself pretty worked up into a major anxiety attack by the time the elevator got down to B. I wished I'd grabbed a shoe to wedge the door open so the elevator wouldn't leave me down there with the wild animals and bad guys and criminals and zombies I was by then sure were all hanging out together, waiting for me in the basement. How could I wedge the door open? Should I have taken a weapon? Is this why Emmett has all the (Nerf) weapons? There was a box on top of the newspaper recycling pile. Perfect. I grabbed it, placed it across the door tracks, and hurdled it with my sack of garbage. It was bright and clean in the basement, like normal when I go down there with an adult. Nobody seemed to be around. I got back to the elevator as the door was trying to close. Ha! Didn't even need that box. I jumped over it and kicked it away.

The door beeped, whining about being made to wait there too long, and closed.

Phew.

Ding. The elevator door opened in the lobby. Mom got in.

"Oh!" she said. "Hi! Were you coming down to meet me?"

"Um, yes!"

"Well, I just need to put down my workbag and go to the bathroom," she said. "Is that okay? Are you in a rush?"

"Nope," I said.

The elevator stopped at 4. Emmett's mom got on.

"Oh, hi!" Mom said to her, too. "Sorry, you caught us going up."

"No problem! I haven't seen you in forever! New haircut?"

Mom ran her fingers through her hair. "Highlights!"

She got highlights? When?

"Looks great," Emmett's mom said. "Really brightens you up!"

"You're so sweet," Mom said as the elevator door closed again. "Sorry to drag you on a detour up to eight. Gracie was meeting me downstairs, but I have to get my act together."

"It's fine. Glad to see you," Emmett's mom said to Mom. And then she asked me, "Are you heading over to Michaela's too?"

I nodded. "I baked some cookies. Is why I didn't go to the game. Or the other game. There's two. At least. Games!"

The moms looked at me like I was unhinged.

I nodded. Fair point.

Eighth floor. *Ding.* The doors opened. The moms said good-bye to each other and made promises to get together for a walk down by the river or for a coffee soon, agreeing that they'd both love that.

"Let me know about Saturday," Emmett's mom called through the closing elevator door. "And don't forget shoes!"

Mom and I looked down at my feet in their socks.

She squinted at me, blinked twice, and waited.

"Good thing you needed a minute," I said. "Oh, and I have to put the cookies I made in a Tupperware!"

"You okay?" Mom asked me.

"I'm fine!" I lied. "Just, yeah! Great!"

"I wanted to ask you about—"

"Mom," I said, more impatiently than I'd intended. "Can we? I just . . . I promised Sienna I wouldn't be late to this party and—"

"Okay," Mom said, and unlocked the door. We hung our keys on their side-by-side hooks and she slipped her shoes off beneath them. I could've flipped the secret don't-automatically-lock thing, I realized. Oh, well.

I found a Tupperware and stacked the fresh-made cookies in it while Mom changed and went to the bathroom. I vowed to myself that I'd be brave and admit what had happened, as soon as she came out. I would say, *Hey, Mom, I have to tell you something: I broke Bret's plate. And threw away the evidence.*

That's why I was in the elevator. Then I'd apologize, and handle however mad she'd get, and, even worse, however sad. She'd never have that treasured plate again, that connection to Bret. I wouldn't pretend it wasn't me who shattered it. I wouldn't take the coward's way out.

"Those look great," she said, crumpling the used piece of aluminum foil I'd left on the counter.

I opened my mouth, but my confession refused to fall out.

She opened the garbage cabinet and pulled out the pail to toss the crumpled silver ball in. No bag. "Ugh," she grumbled. "I hate when Daddy forgets to . . ." She took a deep breath. "*Hate* is an awfully strong word for a lack of garbage bag, isn't it? Well, you're in a rush. We'll deal with garbage bag replacement later. Ready?"

I nodded. Another lie.

39

SO THAT HAPPENED

I spent a long, dragged-out time busily setting up the cookies, taking them out of the Tupperware and arranging them geometrically on three plastic plates, not as nice as Bret's plate but not breakable or important, either. As I slowly pushed the third plate toward the front of the table so people could get at them, I knocked over a partially full cup of soda.

Don't worry about me, all you people, including my best friend, whispering way over there next to the potted trees. Me and the spilled cup of soda both abandoned over here: we're good.

Because I was concentrating on my vital work wiping up the spilled soda, I didn't see AJ approaching until he grabbed some napkins and started wiping up soda with me.

There truly wasn't much soda spilled and it was beading up anyway, but we both scrubbed until that thing was bone dry. And then a bit more. We threw our barely dampened napkins into the trash. So, that was done.

"How's it going?" I eventually asked him as we stood there, just staring into space, where the water towers of the buildings between Michaela's roof and the Hudson were outlined against the pinking sky.

"Great," he said. "Good, great. You? Are these cookies up for grabs? I'm so hungry."

"Oh yeah, absolutely," I said.

He ate one. Fast. He looked like he was going to say something, but instead he took another and popped it into his mouth too, as if they were Doritos. He swallowed, shrugged, smiled sheepishly. "They're good."

"Thanks," I said.

"You made them?"

I nodded.

"Oh."

"Yeah!" I said, too loud. Weirdly overenthusiastic. Shhh.

"They're good."

"Thanks," I said again. "Were you looking for Sienna?"

He blinked his long eyelashes a few times. "Um, no," he said. "You."

My knees wobbled. "Me?"

"I just . . . I was just . . ." He took another cookie and ate it in one gulp, like a snake devouring a mouse. "I was gonna . . . It's kind of a funny . . . The thing is— Emmett!"

"How was the . . . I'm sorry—what?"

"Fine!"

"What?"

"Did you ask, 'How are you?'"

"Oh, um." I tried to rewind the conversation in my mind. "I don't remember."

"I thought . . ." He smiled at me. "Just in case: I'm good, thanks."

I noticed, I thought. But then: *She is my best friend.* "How was the game?" I managed to ask.

"Game?"

"Baseball? About an hour ago?"

"Oh," he said. "Yeah, right—um, good."

"Great!" I said, super psyched. Ugh.

"I mean, we lost, but . . ."

"Oh," I said. I wished we were texting instead. We were better at talking by text, where it all went so smoothly and we were funny together. We picked up each other's references and jokes and rhythms when we were texting and he thought it was Sienna on my end. This talking thing was brutal. What to even say about the fact that he'd lost a baseball game this afternoon? Is that a thing people feel terrible about? Or no biggie? Do you say you're sorry for his loss, or is that only for when somebody dies?

How am I fourteen years old and I still don't know how to have a conversation? "Was it close?" I asked.

"Was what close?"

"The game," I said, sweating. "That you lost." Oh, just

put me out with the trash, will somebody, please?

"No," AJ said. "Uh, not even, no. Nine–nothing. They completely abused us."

I smiled and nodded.

He looked a little confused, justifiably. *Think, Gracie, think. Say something. You can't just smile and nod when somebody says he and his team were completely abused.*

"Hey, yeah, one of my favorite kinds of used," I said. *Please let him get this.*

"Your . . . what?"

"One: Ab," I said. "Two: Conf!"

"Huh?" he asked.

"Favorite kinds of used!" Dying, I explained: "Ab-used. Conf-used."

He blinked a few times. Long eyelashes causing a breeze.

"And, oh," I said, getting slightly louder and maybe also slightly scarier. "Three: Am!"

"Am?"

"Used! Am! Used! Amused! Get it?"

"No."

"Am-used! Hahahaha!" I had to blink away the sweat dripping off my forehead and into my eyes. "Isn't that a great kind of used? To be? Am-used?!"

"Am used?" AJ asked. "Wait, I don't—Who's used?"

"I am," I said. "Hahahaha! Right? Well, you're conf-used. I'm not ab-used, not really, and okay, neither of us is very am-used, obviously! But I am actually used *up*!"

"Okay," he said, stepping one step backward.

Oh, dear God.

I wiped more sweat away from my eyes with my palms, forgetting I'd put on eyeliner and mascara while the cookies were in the oven earlier, until I saw smears of black across my hands.

"Like our favorite kinds of lakes!" I practically shouted. *Why am I screaming?*

"Our what?" he asked.

"Favorite kinds of lakes," I repeated, simply wilting. Other people were coming toward us, the Loud Crowd, marching toward us like an avenging army, to rescue poor AJ from the Crazy Shouting Melting Girl. "Great, Cornf? Lakes? And then you said . . ."

He looked at me, kind of concerned. "What are you talking about?"

"Three: Frostedf," I said. "When you were texting with Sienna. Remember? Late at night? After my birthday party?"

"Oh," he said. He looked embarrassed.

And then it hit me. He hadn't realized I'd seen (never mind written) those texts. He'd been pretending not to understand because he'd thought that it was all a private inside joke, between him and Sienna. Oh no! I'd blown it. Uh-oh. No, no, no. And there was Sienna, almost next to me, finally. Oh no, oh no. I so suck.

"She didn't . . ." I started, then quick, leaning close to AJ to whisper so my best friend wouldn't hear. "I saw Sienna's phone. I read. I didn't mean to. She didn't show me anything private or—"

"It's okay," he said, shaking his head.

"I swear she never . . . It's my fault completely."

"No," AJ said. "I know. It's okay. I just didn't . . . I actually was . . ."

"You okay?" Sienna asked me at exactly the same time as AJ was saying, "It's okay."

"Great," I lied to them both simultaneously.

Sienna squinted at me a tiny bit, unsure.

"Great as a lake," I said. I actually had to close my eyes to ward off the threatening tidal wave of sobbing. I should never go to parties. I just never should.

When I opened them again so nobody would think I'd fallen randomly asleep standing among them, Michaela had latched her arm through Sienna's and was whispering something to her. Sienna nodded her tiny, subtle nod, a single downward head tip. Like a girl in a Renoir painting: so pretty, so perfect.

Michaela turned to AJ and said, all casual, "Hey, AJ, could you do me a favor and run down to my apartment to get some more napkins? We're running low."

"Sure," he said, smiling wide. He's like a golden retriever, eternally up for a task.

"Sienna knows where they are," Michaela added, and gently shoved Sienna toward him.

They went toward the elevator together without looking back at the whispering mass of us. Well, not all of us were whispering. I just stood there, not whispering with anyone but instead watching and wishing good things at my best friend.

Really.

If she was about to go get her first kiss, I wished for it to be not weird but really nice: gentle, sweet, and mutual. As the Loud Crowd moved like one big gossiping amoeba toward the Ping-Pong table, I smiled to myself. That conversation I'd just had with AJ was about a twenty-seven billion on an Awkward Scale of one to ten—completely my fault—but there was an upside: I could feel my crush on AJ lifting a bit.

No. A lot.

I'm not even sure why.

It's not that I suddenly disliked him—not at all. He's great. He's still sweet and good-looking, obviously. But just, suddenly, I could like him in a more normal way. More sturdy, like how I liked him a month ago, before I got all clumsy every time I thought of him. More like how I like enthusiastic Beth, or dorky Dorin, or jokey Harrison, or unnecessarily tall Ricky Wu, despite his unfortunate tendency to do magic tricks. I deeply didn't want to be the one in the elevator with AJ, possibly about to try to kiss. I really didn't. I was happy to have that be Sienna instead.

If anything, I was more jealous of AJ, having time alone with Sienna.

My knees felt normal in their hinges. I wasn't having any trouble balancing on the spinning planet. I could think of AJ and his cute face and his reassuring altitude and sweet attitude and be like, *Yeah, nice guy.*

Yay! Excellent! I could be a noncomplexly good friend again! Thank you, yes, please. Being a good friend is the thing I've actually always liked best about myself. Better than cute toes.

That's why when Riley came over and smiled at me, I smiled back. I had enough good will about everything to spill some over onto her, too. She's probably feeling unchosen, I thought, realizing I was probably the only one of us up there on the roof who knew Riley might be having a hard time right now. Because she was just jealous. Who said that about her one time before?

"Hey," I said. "How're you doing?"

"Me?" Riley asked, flicking her hair.

"Yeah," I said. "You okay?"

"Fine, thanks."

"Yeah," I said, thinking, *Yeah, I get you. Me too.* It felt so good to like everybody again. Even the most difficult among us are really just walking a sometimes rough path, feeling too many feelings all at once. *Be gentle with everybody*, Mom always says; *be gentle and generous.* I used to succeed at that, until last week, which Mom loved about me. And so did I! Welcome back, me! "Same," I said, appreciating the private secrets I shared even with Riley, poor insecure Riley. "Nice night, right? How was the game?"

"It's kind of funny. You didn't even go to the game, but you're here," Riley said.

"Sienna asked me—"

"Oh, you don't have to apologize," Riley said. "Don't get all awkward and defensive again. The last thing we need is a scene, am I right?"

"I . . ." How does she get me so turned around all the time? "I wasn't apologizing. I . . . Sienna wanted me here."

"She invites you to somebody else's party and then she dumps you?"

"She didn't," I said, feeling my face heat up. She did kind of dump me, though, didn't she? No. Kind of? "She and AJ. They went . . ."

"Sure," Riley said, and smiled prettily. "Don't worry about it."

"I wasn't worrying."

"Listen, Gracie. People were talking about you tonight. I thought you should know."

"Talking about me?"

"About who you like."

Sweat, my old enemy. Oh no, oh no, oh no. It would be Riley who realized I liked AJ. Ugh, how perfectly inevitable and hideous.

No.

"Riley, I don't like anybody."

"Come on."

I knew exactly what she was about to say: that just a few minutes ago, when they were all over on the other side of the roof-deck, their whispering was about me and AJ. That everybody except Sienna had seen me flirting with him, and they'd all been commenting on my desperate, sad failed attempts to get AJ to like me instead. After witnessing my betrayal of Sienna, they felt honor-bound to tell her. And so Riley was just the ambassador, letting me know that that's what was about to go down.

Sienna would hate me. Rightly so.

I hated myself for it.

"I don't like him," I said, leaving out the feeble *anymore.*

"It's pretty obvious you do, actually."

"It is?" I asked. "But no, honestly, I don't . . ."

"Admit it! You're totally into Emmett."

"Wait. Emmett?"

"Yeah, Emmett. Don't deny it."

"You think . . . You all think . . . Emmett?"

"Yeah. Obviously you like—"

"No!" I said. Loud, relieved. "I don't like Emmett!"

"You don't?"

"No!" *Shhh.* "We're friends," I whispered. "Just friends."

"Okay," Riley said.

"Youch," Michaela said, beside me.

I'd been in such a fog of trying to figure out how to deny the truth about how I'd been acting toward AJ, I didn't even notice everybody had joined us at the table and they were all devouring the cookies I'd baked. They were also all looking over toward the door, so I did too. Sienna and AJ were coming back onto the roof-deck, and they were holding hands. Emmett was running toward them.

"Hey!" AJ said, big smile all over his face until it faded fast.

Emmett pushed past them.

"Emmett!" AJ yelled, and then turned around and followed him inside.

"What happened?" Beth asked.

Sienna walked straight to the table. "What happened to Emmett?" she asked.

Everybody looked at me.

"I don't know," I said, and stepped closer to Sienna. "How are you?"

"Good," she said. "What was Emmett upset about?"

"Tell us everything," Riley said to Sienna.

Michaela said to me, "I think Emmett heard what you said."

"What did I say?" I asked.

"That you don't like him."

"Gracie!" Sienna gasped. "You said that?"

"I didn't mean *at all*," I spluttered. "I . . . he . . . I said we're friends!"

Michaela shrugged and turned away to talk with David. Riley had swooped in on Sienna by then, and everybody was in a swarm around her. All their backs were toward me.

I pulled out my phone. A text from Mom asking what time I wanted to come home. I ignored that for the moment and texted Emmett: **you okay?**

No answer.

Everybody had moved to the far side of the roof-deck. I was alone with the cookies again. Only seven left.

I texted Mom: **I may head out. kinda done here okay? I'll walk home IT'S FINE**.

Mom texted back immediately: **Stay there. Daddy is at the Starbucks on the corner. He can meet you in the lobby**.

I walked across the roof to the door. Nobody called out to me, so I just ducked my head and kept going.

40

SOME TRUTH

Dad picked me up in the lobby, and after he thanked the doorman, randomly, we walked home up West End Avenue together, past the brownstones and prewar buildings, in the quiet of the evening. I was trying not to be mad, but come on. I am fourteen years old. I can walk eleven blocks by myself.

Couldn't I have ten minutes to myself? I had a lot to think about.

Including the fact that I had texted Sienna and Emmett and even Riley and Michaela to see what had happened and nobody had answered me. I had turned my phone off, sitting on the black leather couch, the doorman pitying me, and then back on.

Nothing.

I smiled at the doorman before I texted Sienna again: **hey sorry I had to go but I want to hear all about what happened <3 <3**

And texted Emmett: **hey srsly you okay?**

Nothing. Very busy here, Mr. Doorman; don't worry about me.

I texted Sienna again, third time in a row with no response: **are you mad at me?**

And then texted Emmett a third time too: **are you mad at me?**

No responses. And then my dad blustered in and explained to the doorman that he was there to pick his daughter Gracie up! And here she is! Hahahaha. I guess we'll head home now. Thank you so much! *Nobody cares, Dad.*

And so while the rest of the grade, or at least the sporty kids, plus Sienna (oh wait, she is kind of a sporty kid, I guess—why did I never realize that before?) and Emmett, stayed at the party on Michaela's roof, I walked grumpily uptown with my father.

It wasn't even fully dark out yet. Dad pointed at the moon in the still-half-bright sky. "Look, a nearly full moon!"

He loves the moon.

I hate the moon. I hate everything.

"It's hovering so big and swollen over the East Side," he said.

"I used to think the sun rose on the East Side," I mumbled.

"The East *Side*?"

I didn't want to get into it. I wanted to just trudge quietly home, feeling like unsorted litter, and crawl into my bed and forget who I am.

"What do you mean?" Dad asked.

"Nothing."

"Gracie."

"I didn't know there was east, like, in the world. Beyond maybe Madison Avenue," I explained unwillingly. "So when you and Mom said the sun rose in the east, I was like, *Oh, sure, east. I remember where that is. It's across Central Park.*"

He laughed a little. I love making Dad laugh.

I could feel my annoyance lift a tiny bit, against my will. "East as a compass direction, instead of, you know, the fancy neighborhood where the museums are? Never occurred to me."

Dad smiled. "Until when?"

"Embarrassingly recently," I said.

Dad smiled at me like I was awesome instead of an idiot.

"Maybe at the Met Museum," I said. "Near all the statues of the naked people, or maybe where the knights are." It's like I'm addicted to making my parents smile. Stop it! Why can't I just be a normal sulky teenager for half an hour?

"That would be where they kept the moon, no?" Dad asked. "With the knights? Get it? Night, knights? They'd keep the moon with the knights?"

I groaned. *Please just leave me alone!*

"I thought that was a good one. Knights and moons."

"Dad! Stop." *Could he please just not push all the time?*

"I'll keep working on it," Dad said. "I'm pretty sure there's a funny joke in—"

"Why didn't you press charges against Bret's killer?"

It was a mean question, and I knew it. I felt mean, but also, like, too bad. I have a right to know. Why is everybody always excluding me?

We walked almost a full block before Dad answered. "It's complicated."

"Didn't you want justice?" I was quoting from an article I'd read.

"Justice." He chuckled but not in a happy way. "That was the lawyer's word. We filed a suit against—"

"But you dropped it."

"Yeah."

"Why?"

"Because it wouldn't . . . Even if we won? If we got a hundred thousand dollars or a million, ten million from her family's insurance company? Would that be justice?"

"I don't know," I said.

"What justice could there be? Our little girl was dead."

I swallowed hard. My anger was wearing off. I couldn't remember why I'd felt like it would be good to torture him like this. Because he sat waiting, reading at a Starbucks down the block from the terrible party I was at, to be available to walk me home? This wasn't helping anything. We crossed even though there were only two seconds left on the walk sign before we started. He usually stops if there are five or fewer.

"Anyway, that's a lie." Dad's voice sounded deeper and growlier than usual, his Boston accent stronger than usual. "I didn't want justice. I wanted vengeance."

I just kept walking next to him, faster and faster, trying to match his long strides. "I don't blame you."

"I blame myself," he said. "It's not a noble feeling, wanting vengeance on a kid."

"A kid?"

"That driver was just a kid herself, twenty years old. Looked down at her phone for a second, maybe. That's what our lawyer said; we could bring it up as a possibility and at least settle with her insurance company. Get a nice amount of money. But how could a 'nice' amount of money pay us back? Our baby was gone. There is not that much money on the planet, nice or otherwise. And meanwhile, the kid was on a suicide watch."

"So you gave up?" I asked. "To protect the driver, since you couldn't protect Bret?"

"No," Dad said. "To protect Mom."

"Mom? From what?"

"If they had put her on the stand, she would've said, *It's not that young woman's fault; it's my fault.*"

Whoa. *What?* "Was it?"

"No," Dad said. "It wasn't. Understand? It was not your mother's fault."

"Okay." I hadn't said it was. The thought had never occurred to me.

"When somebody you love is . . ." he whispered. "She was . . . I couldn't get distracted by lawsuits, or blame. All I could do was pray."

"Pray?" He's an astrophysicist. First time I ever heard him use the word. "For what?" I asked. "For time to reverse itself, tocktick, so Bret—"

"No," Dad said. "It was enough that I was praying to a God I don't believe in. I couldn't pray for the laws of nature to nullify themselves and turn back time."

"I was kind of kidding," I mumbled.

"And certainly I didn't pray for a cash windfall or for that poor girl behind the wheel to suffer. Those are small things, and the universe owed me big."

"So, what, then?" I asked, but then I saw his face, pale and droopy, old-looking. "You don't have to tell me anything else. Sorry."

"No," he said. "Gracie, here's the . . . I'm going to mangle Aeschylus, but. . . . The pain never lets me forget; even in sleep, the despair is an almost unbearable weight on my heart, but drop by drop, through the awful grace of God, or time, sometimes I manage to remember that there's still work to be done. And that even if giving up would be easier for me, easier is not the same as better, and there are people who count on me. So, on we trudge."

"That's it?" I asked. "'On we trudge'? That's your battle cry? Wow."

"Yes. On we trudge. Because people need us, and also, occasionally, we get some proof of the gravity of passing stars detaching planets into interstellar space."

"Sure," I said.

"That's always a good day."

"Okay," I said.

We both turned and started walking again, crossing Broadway at the light and then, at my school, turning uptown.

"You need anything to eat?" Dad asked as we passed the market, its fruit arrayed outside in a rainbow of fresh choices.

"I'm good," I lied.

"How was the party?"

"Not as much fun as the conversation on the way home."

"That bad?"

I half smiled.

"Eighth grade is a rotten time," he said.

"Sometimes," I admitted.

And we walked the rest of the way home together, my phone still as cold and as quiet as a detached planet, or interstellar space, in my pocket.

41

MORE ROTTEN THAN I EVEN REALIZED, ACTUALLY

On my way to school, I passed the homeless woman outside the bank. She's not usually there so early. Neither am I. But I didn't want to risk running into Emmett in the elevator of our building, so I left even earlier than Dad. He let me.

I offered the homeless woman my granola bar.

"You sure?" she asked.

"Absolutely." I don't know where the homeless woman sleeps and wouldn't want to pry. I don't even know her name. I just think of her as the Homeless Woman, like that's the only thing about her. "What's your name?"

"Lina," she answered. "What's yours?"

"Gracie."

"Nice to meet you," she said. "Thanks. This is my favorite kind of granola bar."

"Really?" One thing to feel good about.

"Oh yeah, the best," she said. "Have a great day at school."

"Thanks," I said. "You too."

Ugh. I cannot even have a normal nothing conversation. *You too?* I now have to quit school and run away from home so I won't pass Lina anymore.

When I got to school, nobody was there from our grade, so I scarfed down a crumbly muffin for something to do while sitting among the shiny elementary school babies as they chattered all excited with their parents, pumped up for the coming day. I felt like the BFG, hulking there at the table. Plus, check your privilege: I gave away my breakfast granola bar but within five minutes had my choice of muffins to eat. *I really have no right ever to feel bad about anything*, I reminded myself, unsuccessfully.

The early bell rang. Still no friends. I skulked up the stairs by myself and slumped down in front of my locker.

Sienna hadn't answered any of my texts. I had written a few more last night, and some to Emmett, too, and fallen asleep with my silent phone in my hand, having told nobody about the conversation with my dad. Or anything.

Just before the late bell, a big rush of kids exploded into the eighth-grade area, Sienna in the midst of it. She looked over at me but then lowered her eyes quickly.

We had to go straight into math. But come on. I stood

up and followed her in. "Hey, what did I do?" I asked. "I'm sorry. For whatever it was."

"Nothing," Sienna whispered, and kept walking. She looked so sad.

I followed her. Uncool? Sure. I wasn't likely to make the travel team in Cool, either, even on a good day. And this was already obviously not a good day.

"What? Sienna," I pestered. "Hey."

She put her books down onto her desk and then turned around. "Nothing," she repeated. "You ditched me. But, really, it's fine."

"No," I said. "That's not what . . . I thought . . . you were with . . ."

"I know," Sienna whispered.

"I'm sorry," I said.

"It's okay."

"Okay," I said. But she wouldn't meet my eyes. So I asked, "What?"

"It's not fair," she said.

"That I didn't say good-bye?" I asked. "I said I was sorry, Sienna. I am. I—"

"No," she said. "Not that."

"What, then?"

"Can you, Gracie? Can you let me answer? You're so quick to jump in. I can't even—"

"Okay." I put both hands over my mouth and, behind them, said, "I'm listening."

Sienna smiled, but not like she thought it was funny. "It's

not fair," she whispered, "how much I need you. How much I rely on you for everything, even to write my texts for me. To the point where, if you have to leave a party, it's like my voice leaves with you. So."

"No!" I said too loud. Everybody was looking at us. I lowered my voice. "That's not . . . You don't— I'm sure you were great."

"I wasn't," she said. "I was completely . . . befuddled."

"I'm sorry."

"I have to figure out how to be . . . I kissed a boy last night," she whispered really quietly. "And I've never had a real conversation with him on my own since we started going out."

"You kissed him?"

"Yeah," she whispered.

"How was it?" I asked.

At the same time, she was saying, "But I don't . . . I think we should stop . . ."

"Stop what?" I was so confused. Did AJ do something rude? Did she want to break up with him already? "What happened?"

"We should have more friends than just each other."

"You and AJ?" I realized maybe she felt guilty, like she'd ditched *me*. Which she sort of had. But I didn't want her to worry about me! I was fine! "It's okay. You guys can take a minute or two to yourselves! As long as you don't make a habit—"

"No, Gracie," Sienna interrupted quietly. "Listen. Us. You and me."

"Us?"

"Yes," she whispered. "I'm sorry."

Was she breaking up with *me*? Is that a thing?

I felt like I was in that elevator again, going down, down, down, even though I was just standing there in math, being told to find our seats and let's go over the homework.

"We're . . . but . . ." I said. "We're already friends with everybody."

"You know what I mean," Sienna whispered, and sat down in the seat beside me.

I didn't.

All I heard the whole period was a whooshing noise in my head.

On the way to chorus, AJ was walking up the stairs next to me. I barely noticed. There was just too much thunder in my brain. How was I going to make it through the rest of the day? Or the year? Sienna just broke up with me? *What?*

"Gracie," AJ said. "Gracie."

"Oh," I said, after I figured out that he was talking to me. I didn't know how many times he had repeated my name. "Sorry."

"Did you hear what I said?"

"Sure," I said. "But actually, no."

"I'm breaking a promise by saying this, but I think it's the right thing to do."

"Maybe you shouldn't."

"It's important," he whispered.

"Still," I said, trying not to be mad, trying to smile, but

seriously, if he was going to start telling me truths about Sienna, as if now that he'd been her boyfriend for, oh wow, almost a whole week . . . You know what? Stuff it. She's been my best friend a long time, AJ. You have no idea who she is, what's going on between her and me, what she's feeling. She said herself she's never had a real conversation with you this whole time, so back up, bruh.

"He went out and spent his own money on it that night! He lied when he said he'd already read it. He'd never even heard of it before."

"What?" I asked. "Who?"

"He spent his own money he earned from opera to buy it at Bank Street Book Store."

AJ's face was all red. We were at the door of chorus.

"I don't know what you're talking about."

"You gotta ask yourself why he would do that, right?" AJ asked. "And read the whole thing that night? The whole book. He says he's like the peacocks."

"What? Peacocks? What are you—"

"Plus, he always makes sure he's on your gym team. And then you do that to him, in front of everybody?"

"Emmett?"

"Yeah," he said, looking at me like I was the one not making sense.

"I didn't mean anything!" I said. "Riley asked. I wasn't—"

"I used to think of you as maybe the nicest person I knew," AJ whispered. "And in the top four or five coolest. I was even jealous, because sometimes it seems like you're almost maybe better friends with Emmett than I am. And he's my best friend. But I would never dis him like you did last night."

AJ rushed into chorus, leaving me in the hall. Emmett was standing in the front of the boys' section, serious, studious, looking over the music I knew he'd already memorized. On top of his pile of books, beside him, was his shiny copy of *Brown Girl Dreaming.*

Shiny and new.

I took two steps backward and crashed into Ms. Hall, the chorus teacher. I mumbled some excuse about being sick and then rushed down the stairs, away from chorus and toward the nurse's office, but then, since I wasn't actually sick, I veered off into the girls' bathroom on the second floor.

I slammed myself into the far stall. I dropped my stuff onto the floor, locked the door behind me, and just stood there, my head pressed to the metal door, trying to stop existing.

42

APPROXIMATING

Solve for *x*?

Solve for ex.

Sienna has plenty of right to be mad at me for flirting with her boyfriend. So even though she's breaking up with me for the wrong reason, I can't be upset, because what am I going to do, correct her? *No, Sienna, what you should actually be mad about is* . . . Uh, no. Never. Gonna. Happen. I owe her a cosmic debt for having been a bad friend; I deserve anything she does to me.

And Emmett actually has every right to be mad at me too. All he's ever done is be the most awesome friend: fun, funny, literally always on my team (until today), always acting like I'm great, and he gets me and likes me and apparently (wait, really?) even spending his own money on a book and reading it all in one night (why? Not sure I follow that whole thing—what happened there?), and then, from his (incorrect but still) point of view, I turn around and announce to everybody that I don't like him. That is so not what I meant. Stupid Riley was asking a whole different, embarrassing question! If he would just stop turning away from me and not listening, I could explain.

He'd laugh. He'd be like, *Oh,* that's *what she was asking? Hahahaha*. And then he'd say something so perfect and funny, and everything would be fine.

Not that I should be mad at him, for ignoring me. Obviously not. What would being angry even accomplish? Last time I got angry, it was at Riley, and that accomplished zero. I'm not mad. I'm sorry. For everything. But otherwise fine!

I'm fine.

I am always fine.

Show your work.

I am turning in a social studies quiz with three out of ten answers filled in, and those answers are actually just nonsense and crossed-out names of the two people I like best in the world. So. Checking my answer? Not *completely* fine.

Approximately the opposite of fine.

43

BROKEN

When I finally got home, the one thing I'd been wanting to do all day, Mom was So. Much. Wanting to know how my day was. If I had a lot of homework. If I had plans with Sienna over the weekend. If I wanted to go Saturday night to see the opera Emmett was in.

What?

"They have an extra ticket because Daphne has a thing," Mom said, following me down the hall to the kitchen. "And Emmett wants you to come!"

"No, he doesn't," I said.

"His mom told me," Mom said, putting her arm around me. "I think it's sweet!"

"Mom."

"You should probably wear a dress," she said.

"No."

"Does your blue dress still fit?"

"Mom!"

"We could go shopping tomorrow. It's from the fall, that blue dress, and you've grown since then. You probably don't fit in those black pumps anymore either."

"None taken." There were banana muffins fresh made and waiting all invitingly on a plain white plate. My mom makes the best banana muffins, usually when she has an article due or is tense about something. But usually they're arranged on Bret's plate. Ugh.

I bypassed them and grabbed a store-bought chocolate chip cookie from a package in the cabinet, as self-punishment. I shoved it hard into my mouth, a not-polite nibble. Tough. I obviously wasn't going to have to squish into that blue dress anyway.

Mom scrunched her shoulders up toward her ears, grinning. "It's your first date!"

"No!" I yelled, accidentally spitting out a couple of cookie crumbs. "Ew! Mom! It's so not!"

"Maybe not officially, but in a way it is!"

"Mom! Stop!" I shoved the rest of the cookie into my open mouth and pushed past her. I dashed up the hall toward my room, trying not to choke on the stale cookie shards clogging my throat. I wanted to stop in the hall bathroom to spit the gross mess out in the toilet, but my mother was following me.

"Gracie, what's wrong?"

"Please leave me alone," I grumbled incomprehensibly through cookie bits.

She was right behind me, so I couldn't close my door. We stood on the two sides of the threshold of my room, me inside, her out in the hall. Lightning was hiding in the corner next to my bookcase. I so related. Where is a boot for me to shove my head down into?

Mom leaned against my doorframe. "Daddy said you had some questions about Bret."

"Mom. No. I don't," I begged. I just needed to be alone. "Sorry, I have a lot of homework I need—"

"It's only four o'clock, Gracie!" She laughed, in honestly the most judgy way. I am not just saying that to justify what happened next. It was that little snorting nose-exhale non-laugh laugh of hers. Like she was saying, *It's midafternoon, Gracie; why would you be doing homework now? Why aren't you on any sports teams like the cool kids, you cloddish loser?*

"I know what time it is. Thanks."

"You can't spare two minutes to chat with your mom?"

"Mom!" I took a deep breath, trying not to explode. "I really want to get started on—"

"I made some banana muffins. Come have a snack," she said. "Do you know where the handprint plate is, by the way? I couldn't find it."

"No!" I said. Well, shouted.

"Oh . . . kay," she said in a completely suspicious way.

"What?" I yelled. "What do you even want from me?"

"Gracie," she said. "What's going on?"

"Nothing!"

"Well, I don't like your tone of voice."

"No? Too bad!"

"Excuse me?"

"What?" I yelled. "I'm obnoxious? I'm loud? Yeah, I am. You can say it. I know that's what you're thinking, what you're always thinking. I'm not perfect like Bret. Second prize! You had a good one the first time, but now you're stuck with a big, oafish, loud, sweaty screw-up who doesn't do sports!"

"What? Gracie!"

"I broke it! Isn't that what you're implying? Fine, Sherlock—you win! I broke it, and I threw away the pieces. I admit it. Happy?"

"What are you talking about?"

"Bret's plate! If you want to accuse me, just go ahead and accuse me! Stop looking at me all bug-eyed!"

"You broke the plate?" Mom asked.

"It was an accident!"

"The plate with her handprint on it? In blue? And her name?"

"I'm sorry," I said, every muscle tensed. *Please don't be mad,* I silently prayed.

She didn't respond.

I wished I had continued taking the coward's way out. Who was I trying to kid? I'd rather be unblamed than brave. Tocktick. Please? She could look around for the plate, ask Dad if he'd seen it, and I'd stay silent and ashamed.

Nope. Ticktock. Too late.

"What . . ." Mom's voice was small and unrecognizable, like a child's. "What happened?"

"I just . . . I took it out yesterday, and I was trying to be careful, but then I . . . I don't know what happened. I just . . . It smashed on the floor into powder and pieces, and I can't . . . I'm sorry. I'm really sorry, Mom."

"It's okay," Mom said, still in that baby voice, not looking at me. "Accidents happen."

"No! It's not okay!" *Wait, what?* I was all tangled up.

"Gracie!"

"You can be mad at me, Mom!"

"It's a plate." She shrugged. "What's done is done."

"Mom! You loved that plate! Don't lie! I know you're mad!"

"Gracie, being mad won't change—"

"It was Bret's handprint! I smashed it after you took such special care of it my whole life and I broke it and why didn't you ever take me to make a handprint plate?"

"What?"

"Nothing."

"Did you— Gracie, did you smash the plate on purpose?"

"No!" I yelled.

"Because you were jealous?" Mom asked. "Of Bret?"

"No!"

Her eyes narrowed. "It sure sounds to me like you smashed that plate on purpose, to hurt me for some reason!"

"I have to go," I said.

"Go where?"

I didn't know. "I just need . . . please. Please. Please just . . . I'm . . . I want to take Lightning out to the park."

"What?"

I dashed to my closet and dumped the too-small pair of black pumps out of their shoe box onto the floor. *I don't need pumps; I'm obviously disinvited from the opera, Mom. News flash. Nobody likes me anymore, including you. Including Emmett.*

At my desk, I stabbed a pen through the shoe box lid while my mother watched, her face all cartoonishly concerned. Save it. I stabbed and stabbed the pen through the lid to make air holes for my tort so she wouldn't suffocate like I felt I might.

"Gracie," Mom said again. "I don't know what just happened. What's—"

"I'm just going to the park!" I said. "If I had a normal pet like a dog, I'd be walking it in the park every day, by myself. Like any normal fourteen-year-old. But instead I just stay home all the time like a pitiful baby. I don't do any sports after school because of you! Because you want me to come straight home every day!"

"I don't want you to—What?"

"Yes, you do! Because you're paranoid I'm gonna die! So I don't get to be on a team or have a dog. I have a tortoise! You can't even cuddle a tortoise. But fine! I have a tortoise! Hooray. I'm taking it out for a fricking walk!"

I grabbed Lightning and shoved her into the box. She skittered around in it, surprised to be in there, awakened from her nap and body-slammed into lady-shoe jail.

"Ah no," Mom said, blocking my doorway. "I don't think you are, young lady."

"Watch me." I slammed the cover onto the shoe box.

"Gracie! This is so unlike you!"

"No, it's not!" I said, grabbing my sneakers from near her slipper-wearing feet. "This is exactly like me!"

"Well, I don't know what's going on with you, but you're not storming out of here like—"

"Like what?" I shoved my feet into my sneakers without untying them, which I know drives Mom nuts because it crushes the backs, but too bad; I didn't even care anymore. "Like a person? Like a normal teenager instead of a cartoon Bitmoji of Sunshine Girl? Gah!" I grabbed the box with Lightning in it and faced Mom. *I'm a tiny bit taller than she is*, I realized. *If I look straight ahead, my eyes hit her forehead*. I squinted down at her.

"Gracie." She reached out to touch my arm. Like stupid Riley did. I yanked away and maybe slammed poor Lightning into the side of the box.

"Stop it!" I yelled.

Mom flinched.

"I've been so scared of making you mad, Mom—or sad, disappointing you in any way my whole life, I've become you! Never mad, never sad, never anything but fine! Well, guess what! I'm not fine and neither are you!"

I yanked my necklace down by the yellow stone, because it had twisted around and was choking me. The chain pulled hard on the back of my neck, cutting into it, and then snapped. A few little pieces of metal sprinkled down on the floor, and the yellow part sank in my hand. I tossed it toward the shoes. Whatever. Good-bye to it. I didn't care.

"Gracie!" Mom was yelling.

I pushed past her, Lightning in the shoe box, grabbing my keys off the hook on my way out the door. Maybe I pushed Mom a little more roughly than I meant to.

"Gracie!" Mom yelled, rubbing her arm. "Get back here this minute!"

"No!" I yelled as I dashed down the stairs.

"Gracie!" Mom yelled after me. "Don't you dare storm out of this . . . Gracie! Gracie Grant, you get back here now! Gracie!" I heard my name echoing in the stairwell as I raced down, down, down, away from her, away from the sticky net she was trying to catch me in.

Failing.

She couldn't catch me in it, couldn't keep me in.

I was gone.

44

ALONE, OR, CAREFUL WHAT YOU WISH FOR

Lightning was so fast in the grass, down in Riverside Park. I'm not saying that as an excuse. She just looked so happy, is all I'm saying. When I took her out of the shoe box and set her down on the grass, she froze, like *What?* Then she looked around—left, right, left again, like, *Wait, seriously? I had no idea! There's all this? And I get to be in it?*

She started sprinting across the field of green, stopping for a few seconds to sample the clover, then off again. I smiled and watched her, my reptile role model. I didn't care that the seat of my jeans was getting a bit damp from last night's rain left over on the ground. Who was going to see me anyway? The sky was crystal blue, the grass was electric green, my tortoise was happier than ever. And then my phone buzzed.

Yes!

Emmett? Sienna?

Mom.

Texting that it was not okay in our family to storm out like that and I better come home right now, and then asking me to at least let her know where I am, then at least that I am okay.

I held the phone, staring at it. Willed myself to answer. No reason to torture her. Answer, Gracie. Just say, *I'm fine. Be home soon.*

What can I say in my own defense? I just wanted the minute, as awful as that seems. As awful as it *is*. I just wanted the minute.

I was picturing the woman at the Hungarian Pastry Shop, sitting there all alone with her book and her tea, her yellow necklace (in my mind anyway) and her bitten croissant, owning the day in a way I have never owned a day, not a single minute of a day. I always have to either be within reach of my parents' fingertips or at least have a signed permission slip. To assure them that I'm fine. I'm safe. I'm not dead.

I never get to just be.

Alone.

Actually fine.

I never realized how much oxygen that took up until I was sitting there, just looking up at the near-cloudless blue sky through the gaudily pink tree above me, and then noticing how the sky spread itself, smooth as blue frosting, over the dark Hudson River. So much sky. To my right, all the way up past the George Washington Bridge; to my left, down past the skyscrapers of Midtown and Downtown and, beyond them, to the ocean. Endless sky. Sky's the limit. Sky forever upward but not forever down; down only to me. Because where's the bottom of the sky? Right here where I am. The only end point of the sky is the top of the ground. From the ground up, I realized, is all sky. So, even as I slumped there in the damp green grass, I was sitting in the sky.

Sitting in the sky and catching my breath. Breathing in and out, easily, watching the one poof of a cloud float its lazy solo way north toward the bridge.

Free.

Like me, for this one time, this first time. Just sitting there, leaning back on my elbows, by myself and *actually* okay, not pretending to be okay or acting okay so that nobody would have to worry about me. Not automatically quickly saying, *I'm fine!* because that's what I have to say to make sure nobody is stressed. I closed my eyes and smelled, really smelled the nose-tickling herbiness of the grass and the slightly overdoing-it perfume of maybe that pink blossomy stuff in the branches above me. Actually *used* my senses. Not faking it, like usual.

I started laughing a little, realizing I was thinking, *Wait. Seriously? I had no idea! There's all this? And I get to be in it?*

My phone buzzed again. I opened my eyes to check.

DAD: Not okay, Gracie. Text your mother NOW.

I took a deep breath.

Then another.

I closed my eyes and just smelled the spicy sweetness again, just that. Just smell.

Just a minute. One minute all for myself.

So selfish.

Shhhh. One more breath.

Okay. I opened my eyes, picked my phone back up, and started a new text to both of my parents.

me: I'm fine I just need a half hour or so. I'm in the park I'll come home soon. you can punish me or whatever you want then. sorry. ILYSM.

I held my phone and stared at it. Waiting. It didn't take more than a few seconds before the dreaded three pulsating dots showed.

MOM: No, Gracie. Not half an hour. Not ten minutes. Now.

DAD: Where are you?

Ugh, I thought. I just told you; I'm in Riverside Park. I'm fine. I'm safe. I am just sitting on the green grass with the bluest endless sky around and above me and the joggers sweatily racing past, and the river, oblivious, flowing in both directions beyond that.

I. Am. Fine.

One breath for myself; then I'll respond. Two more breaths. One. Two.

Okay. Just want to close my eyes for one minute and take one more breath, just me, alone and fine, not answering to anybody, even the damp grass beneath me. Okay. But no apologies this time. Be strong, Gracie. Not sorry. Actually *fine.*

me: you guys I'm in Riverside Park down near the water just past 105th I think? I'm fine I'll be home soon. okay?

One last look around at the freedom of being out here alone. Well, not alone. Me and my tortoise.

Wait.

Where is . . .

Oh no.

Lightning was nowhere.

Lightning was gone.

45

LOST

on my way! I texted my parents.

I pushed the heels of my hands into my eyes and tried to blot the tears out, and the sunshine, too. Ugh, how had this happened? Why was I so muddleheaded and irresponsible and selfish? Was this, like, divine punishment for taking five minutes to myself? For paying attention only to my own self for five selfish minutes?

Or something bigger?

For liking AJ, which I don't even anymore? For being rude to my mother?

For growing up?

For growing up and taking it for granted, when my older

sister who is half my age now and stuck there never got to grow up?

Fine! *Sorry!* Okay? Is that what you want, God or universe or fate? *Sorry.* I'm sorry. Whoever is hiding my tortoise from me, to make this point? I suck—I admit it. Please show me where Lightning is. Please don't kill an innocent tortoise just because I'm horrible.

I picked up the empty shoe box and lid, searching around frantically. A hawk circled overhead. Don't hawks eat tortoises? I could picture it so clearly. This is how I'd find Lightning: the hawk would swoop down to grab Lightning, and I'd see her the second before the hawk got her in his beak, too late. I scanned the whole patch of grass. No torts. Maybe she'd ventured onto the path and gotten run over by a biker? No smooshed torts that I could see. Maybe she kept going across the path and then over the edge onto the rocks or into the Hudson? Would a tortoise know not to do that? They are *land animals.* They have to have some instinct not to do that, right?

Sure, a tortoise who gets stuck head-down in a boot probably has awesome instincts out in the wild world.

Plus, honestly, how big could her brain be inside that tiny head of hers? Like, the size of a pea at most? A sesame seed? She's obviously a genius among tortoises, but still, the bar is necessarily low. No offense! Oh, Lightning, where are you?

Please come back. I promise anything. I won't demand independence ever again. Or I will be more responsible. I won't be jealous. I'll be a better friend. Or I'll be more honest. I'll never eat a croissant or wish for one or . . .

MOM: I'm not angry, sweetheart. I just want to understand what's going on.

Maybe I should disappear too?

No. Bad idea. Also, not one of my skills. I have to go home. On we trudge. I have to tell them what happened, what I did, after they finally let me have a pet, one week later and this. Admit it, and let them see the real, horrible, irresponsible disaster zone I am.

And ask them not to forgive me but to help me find her.

Quick. Before it's too late.

I hurried up the steps toward the street.

People stared and then looked away. It's New York City. Everybody has seen way weirder stuff than an overgrown weeping girl with a big nose and an empty shoe box, gulping and snuffling her tripping way up Riverside Drive.

me: sorry sorry sorry almost home

Luckily we have no doorman in our building, so unlike in Sienna's and Michaela's, there's nobody to fake-smile at, no fancy men in their crisp uniforms to say hello, hello to, like a parrot on a perch. There's just the heavy door you pull open, and then the even heavier second door you unlock and push open. You can keep sobbing and drooling and leaking your nose goo or whatever other disaster is happening to your face all the way across the lobby without anyone to fake okay for, and for another minute just be the hot mess you truly are.

Into the elevator.

But then, at the last second, literally—after I pressed 8 and slumped against the elevator's back wall as the door slid shut, I jolted upright and pressed 4.

Emmett hadn't answered my texts, and hated me.

Still: *Please be home, Emmett. Please.*

46

NOT LIKELY TO MAKE TRAVEL CHARADES TEAM EITHER

Emmett's sister, Daphne, answered the door. "Wow, come in," she said. "You okay?"

I shook my head and showed her the empty shoe box. I was having trouble catching my breath.

"You need to borrow shoes? You lost your shoes?"

I kept shaking my head, and, to my shame, crying harder.

"Were you mugged? Did somebody steal your shoes? Gracie, what happened?"

I just gasped in response. No words. The worst round of charades ever.

"Emmett! Gracie's here." Daphne put her arm around me, guiding me into their hallway, past the small table covered with their mom's decorative candles. I hunched over, gulping air.

Emmett opened his door and peeked out, his face grim until he saw me. I must've looked as bad as I felt, because his anger melted instantly into concern.

"What happened?" he asked.

I tried to answer but failed.

"She can't talk," Daphne said.

I honestly couldn't breathe in *or* out, though I was kind of panting really fast, like a dog after a hard run. I was trying to tell them both I was fine, just needed a second, but also that Lightning was lost—help, help—but don't worry; everything is fine! All that came out of my mouth was a strangled gasping sound.

I sank onto their hall rug. Daphne sat on one side of me, and Emmett sat on the other. I gasped and sobbed, between them. They didn't ask me any more questions, including the obvious one (had a zombie recently bitten me?), just sat there until Emmett eventually asked, "Is that your phone buzzing?"

I took it out of my pocket and handed it to him. His thumbprint is the third key to my phone's security, so he unlocked it.

"Your mom seems kind of upset," Emmett whispered, close to my face. "Runs in the family, clearly."

That made me laugh a tiny bit, which weirdly let me then breathe in a full gulp of delicious air. Phew. In that moment of relief, I realized I was also damp with sweat.

Because, #sweatyguys.

"What do you want me to tell her?"

I snorted big and wiped my embarrassing nose on my

sleeve. I looked into Emmett's sweet worried face and whispered, "I lost Lightning."

"What?" he asked. "Where? Maybe she's head-down in a boot again."

"No," I said. "In the park."

"She's in the park?"

"Yeah."

"Crap." Emmett stood up and ran into his room.

"Gimme," Daphne said gently, holding out her hand for the phone, which Emmett tossed to her as he went. She asked me, "Do you want me to text your mom and explain?"

I shook my head. Everything was wrecked, though I could breathe again, a little. I seemed unlikely to die on their hall rug in the next few seconds. So, some good news.

Depending on your interpretation of the word *good.*

And your opinion of me.

"How about if I say you're here, at least?" Daphne asked. "Your mom is panicking, seems like. Wow. She's fast at texting."

Emmett stood in from of me, holding his phone, his shoes on and untied as always. "Let's just go up and tell your mom what happened and then we'll run back to the park and find Tempus. Come on." He put out his hand for mine and yanked me off the floor. "Let's go."

He pulled me toward his door.

"I don't know what to do," I mumbled.

"Yeah, you obviously do," he said, texting on his phone. "Ugh, this elevator is the slowest thing in the world."

"I fully don't," I argued. "Oh! I forgot the shoe box."

"It's okay," Emmett said. "I'll text Daphne. She'll bring it and meet us in the lobby."

"She doesn't have to."

He just kept texting. The elevator door opened. We stepped in.

"If we don't find Lightning, we won't need the shoe—"

"Where in the park?" Emmett asked without looking up from his phone.

"Riverside Park." I slumped against the elevator's back wall.

"Yeah. Where?"

"I don't . . ." I closed my eyes. I was more tired than I'd ever been in my life.

"Where? Gracie."

I didn't open my eyes. "You know how you go in at One Hundred and Eighth?"

"Yeah. Then left? Past the dog run? Or up toward Fairway?"

"Left, then down by the water."

"That patch of grass before the tennis courts?" he asked. "With the pink tree?"

"Yeah." I'd never noticed the pink tree before today. How did he know? I looked at him. He kept texting. I closed my eyes again, but *ding*: 8.

Emmett pushed me out. My mother opened the door before we even got to it. Dad was standing right behind her. "Gracie," Mom said. "What the . . ."

"Lightning got away," Emmett said. "We have to go to the park to find her."

"Oh no," Mom said.

"I can't . . . I think . . . I . . ." I was crying again. I didn't even have a plan for what to say. I just wanted to curl up into a ball and go to sleep and wake up and this would all have been a bad dream. I leaned against the Never Gonna Happen door.

"Let's go," Mom said.

"I'm sorry," I managed while she stomped into her shoes without first untying them.

"Later," Mom said. "You can be sorry later. Let's go."

"Where are my glasses?" Dad asked.

"On your face," Mom said. "Keys."

Dad grabbed keys. I turned around to look for Emmett. He was back at the elevator, pressing the down button. By the time Dad got his loafers on, the elevator door was sliding open. The four of us rode down in grim silence.

"How did you lose Lightning?" Dad asked.

"Shhhh," Mom said. "Later."

Daphne was in the lobby, holding the empty shoe box and my phone, wearing running shoes. "Let's go," she said, handing over my phone.

"Thanks." I sprinted ahead with her toward Broadway and across to the park.

"Careful," Mom called after us, but we were already across.

"We'll meet you there!" Emmett yelled.

47

LOST AND FOUND AND LOST

I showed Daphne the spot where I'd last seen Lightning. "Okay," she said. "I'll walk up the hill looking. You walk down." She placed the shoe box on the ground to mark where I'd been sitting.

"Let's do a grid search!" Emmett yelled, running toward us down the path ahead of my parents.

"A what?" Daphne asked.

"That's what this website suggests," Emmett said, holding up his phone. "We get as many people as possible and split the area into a grid, or a circle and then, you know, like a pie chart, we each take a slice."

"Or like a pie," I said.

"A what?" Daphne asked.

"Pies are even nicer than pie charts," Emmett said. "*Pie* comma *easy as*."

"If you look it up in the index," I said.

"Exactly." Emmett tucked his phone into his pocket. "We'll find her."

"I don't know," Dad said. "You have to prepare yourself that we—"

Mom touched his sleeve. "Shhh," she said. "Take your slice and start looking."

"I'm looking, I'm looking," Dad said as Emmett pointed him diagonally up the hill to the left.

He pointed me down the hill, to the right. I went, stepping carefully, scanning the grass. Emmett took the slice of ground beside me. I heard him whispering his names for her. "Frightening, Light-Year, Tempus," he whispered.

I don't even know if tortoises can hear.

I heard, though.

I turned toward him and saw Sienna running down the hill toward us.

"What are you doing here?" I asked, but Emmett was telling her where to look, explaining the slice idea. Meanwhile, Michaela and Beth ran toward us on the jogging path from the other direction, holding their tennis racquets over their shoulders.

"We came for the tortoise hunt!" Beth yelled.

"Emmett said your tortoise escaped?" Michaela asked.

I nodded.

Emmett sent them down toward the rocks, across the path, to search there. I tried not to picture Lightning lying broken and smashed there, and Beth and Michaela devastated to discover her, wishing for the rest of their lives they'd kept working on their backhands instead.

I lowered my eyes and kept looking.

"Hey!" Dorin called, from the path above. She was on her scooter, her helmet tightly buckled under her chin.

"Hey!" I called back. "Dorin, you're here?"

She ignored the ridiculousness of that question. She dropped her scooter and stepped over it, pointing. "Has anybody looked for the speed demon in these bushes yet?"

"No," Emmett said.

"I'll take them," Dorin said.

"Good call."

I took a second to stop searching for Lightning and looked around instead. My parents, Emmett, his sister, Sienna, a couple of girls from school I didn't even think were my real friends—all hunched-over Quasimodos, silently searching, as if they'd lost their mother's diamond in the dirt.

"Thank you," I whispered in Emmett's direction.

He didn't respond. I don't know if he heard.

The sun was heading toward the tops of the buildings on the Jersey side of the river. If we were going to find Lightning, I thought, we probably would have by now.

If it got dark, we'd all have to go home. Maybe we'd try again in the morning, or after school. Lightning would have to spend the night out in the park alone. Or, worse, not alone.

With the bad guys and predators and who knows what else?

"Well, this is interesting," Dorin called from deep in the bushes. I looked over but couldn't see her. Just bushes.

"What's interesting?" Emmett yelled.

"I can't be sure this is the correct tortoise, but there is definitely a Russian tortoise here with a lot of go in her."

We all ran up the hill toward her voice. She was deep in the bushes, crouched down in a squatting position, her helmet still on but unbuckled now. And there was Lightning, sitting on Dorin's sneaker.

"That's her," I whispered, and started to cry again.

Sienna's arm grabbed me around the waist.

"I think she thought I was you," Dorin said. "Must be the sneakers. I got the same ones as yours yesterday. See? They really are comfortable, Gracie, you were right. My half brother? He's so adorable? He said the most hilarious thing, that they look like clown shoes? But I—"

I wasn't listening. I was leaning past her and grabbing Lightning and holding her up for everybody to see.

They all cheered, even Michaela and Beth, coming up the hill, still holding their racquets, and Mom and Dad, raising their arms into the air.

"You guys are the best," I said to them all. "All of you."

"None taken," Dorin said. "Since I'm the one who found her."

"I'm the one who called everybody," Emmett protested.

"We blew off our tennis lesson," Michaela said.

"I ran up from Eighty-Fourth Street," Sienna said.

"Well, I'm the one who lost her," I said. "So, other than me, you guys are seriously all amazing."

"Well, if you hadn't lost her, we wouldn't've had the chance to prove it," Emmett said.

I hugged Lightning. She looked at me like, *Dude, I'm still a tortoise.*

So I put her back down on the grass. She headed toward the bushes again. "Uh, no. No freaking way," I said, and grabbed her up again. Beth laughed. Michaela asked Dorin to show them where exactly she'd found Lightning, while Daphne held out the shoe box and I placed her, gently this time, inside.

"Let's go home," Mom said. "Thank you, everybody."

We all said our good-byes.

"I'll text you later," Sienna said. "See how you're doing."

"Thank you," I said.

I could hear my friends chattering behind me about how scared they'd been that they wouldn't find Lightning, or that they'd find her dead. Mom and Dad kept shooting each other knowing glances and rubbing my back. I knew there was going to be a lot to discuss when we got home.

"I want to thank Emmett," I told them. They nodded, so I caught with Emmett and Daphne. "Thanks," I said. "Seriously."

"No problem," Daphne said.

"You texted everybody?" I asked Emmett.

"One of the websites I found said to gather as many people as possible to do a grid search, so—"

"I didn't even think of . . . I was so scared."

"Sure," Emmett said. "Promise this wasn't just your feeble attempt to get out of racing Spark Plug against Fluff?"

"Did you see how far Lightning got?" I asked, trash-talking right back, so relieved to be able to be happy. "No way Fluff stands a chance. Lightning was supposed to be an ironic name, not an accurate one."

"We'll see," Emmett said. "Fluff can be fast when he wants to be."

"My money's on the speed-demon tortoise," Daphne said, and then put her earbuds in.

We clomped up the stone steps out of the park behind Daphne, ahead of my parents. Lightning was scratching at the sides of the shoe box, eager to regain her freedom. Ha. No.

"I wasn't kidding," I whispered to Emmett as we got to the top.

"About what?" He looked suddenly serious.

"That I completely didn't know what to do."

"Oh, that," he said. "You did so."

"I fully didn't."

"You did!" He shrugged. "You came to get me."

I opened my mouth to say something back, but there were no words.

48

OKAY

We put Lightning in the bin, which she resented after all that park freedom, but tough darts. I lay down on my bed and waited. My parents didn't come and didn't come. I knew I was in trouble and they were going to Have a Talk with me.

I was so tired, I just stared at the ceiling, wondering, by habit, what Bret would advise me if she were alive. I couldn't think of a thing. I silently thanked her, in case she was actually my guardian angel as well as imaginary friend, and had pointed me toward Emmett, Emmett toward Dorin, and Dorin toward Lightning.

"Gracie?" Bret said. I might've been starting to fall asleep because I was pretty sure Bret was standing in my doorway, calling my name.

"Mm-hmm?" I responded, half dreaming, maybe, not wanting her to leave.

"Get some sleep," she said. "Everything's gonna be okay."

"Okay," I answered.

And I didn't wake up till morning.

49

NOT SO SLOW, NOT SO QUIET

All day people were talking about Lightning. Sienna sat between Michaela and Beth at lunch, which felt like a punch in my heart. But there it is. I sat at the end of the table between Harrison and Dorin. Still, I smiled and didn't cry.

Cute toes. Live tortoise.

Michaela and Beth had everybody laughing, telling about their search down by the Hudson, so scared the crumpled thing that ended up being just a takeout container was dead Lightning and so relieved when Dorin called out from inside the bushes.

"How do you even lose a tortoise?" Riley asked, rolling her eyes.

Nobody answered her. She clearly felt left out that she didn't get a text inviting her to search. And when Riley feels bad, watch out.

Sienna gave me a micro headshake. I did the same back.

That's something, I told myself.

Awesome Ms. Washington called us all into the gym for dodgeball. As we walked in, Riley leaned toward Sienna and said, "I mean, how slow do you actually have to be, to lose a tortoise? Right? LOL. Just saying."

"How insecure do you actually have to be, to be so nasty?" Sienna asked in her usual calm quiet voice. "Right? Just saying."

Riley stopped and stared at Sienna, her hand on her slender hip. "Excuse me?"

Dorin stepped between them, smiling broadly. "Actually some Russian tortoises can be very fast. You might be surprised. Many reptiles—"

"Ew," Riley said to Dorin. "You're a reptile."

"Stop embarrassing yourself, Riley," Sienna said, loud enough for everybody to hear.

"I'm not the one who—"

"Yes, you are," Sienna said. "You're always the one who."

"What does that even—You're just trying to show off for AJ, now that you—"

"No, Riley, I'm not trying to show off for anybody. I'm just bored of your nasty pettiness. Everybody is."

Riley looked around at us. I nodded. Emmett nodded,

and AJ nodded. Michaela and Beth both nodded too.

"You're just jealous," Riley said, her cheeks burning red. "All of you."

"Nobody's jealous of you," Dorin said.

"We just think you're kinda pathetic," Sienna said.

"Well," Riley said. "I don't . . . You're all just . . ." And she ran out of the gym.

Nobody ran after her.

We rocked at dodgeball after that, all of us. Emmett and I were on the same team again. We lost, but it was close.

50

ENOUGH

"Let's go to the market," Mom said when I got home.

I said okay. I wasn't sure if I was in trouble or what. Usually Dad does the grocery shopping, and Friday nights we often go out for Korean or Indian food, maybe sushi, occasionally tapas. I wasn't asking, though.

We wandered through Westside Market, quietly choosing things. We waited in line and I bagged while Mom said, "Credit," and signed the slip. We each carried two bags full of food out of the store.

"I didn't mean to do it," I said, passing the flower selection.

"Which thing?"

"Bret's plate," I said. "I didn't break it on purpose. I mean, obviously I didn't mean to lose Lightning, either. Or yell at you."

"Okay," she said.

"Are you mad?" I asked.

She didn't answer right away.

"It's okay if you are."

"I'm a little sad," Mom said. "I loved that plate."

"I know you did," I said. "I'm sorry. About everything."

She took my hand. "We could make one with your hand if you want," she said.

"That's okay," I said. "My big paw? Too weird."

"I love your hands," she said, holding it up to admire it by the light of the pizza shop we were passing, the one we never go to. "They're so strong, and so beautiful."

Which made me cry. Seriously. I started to cry because my mother said my hands are strong and beautiful. I don't know why. Getting to be a habit. What is wrong with me? Too bad there's not a travel crying team. I could be a starter.

At our corner, we walked past the pale neon light from the diner sign that tourists stand under to take pictures of one another, because some old TV show was filmed there. "Let's sit for a sec," Mom suggested at the steps of the building next to ours.

"Okay."

Mom sat beside me, her hand warm on my back, not rubbing, just imprinting; I could feel it through my T-shirt. Our bags were lined up in front of us like pawns.

"Do you know why Bret ran out into the street that day?"

"Chasing a ball?"

"She was mad at me," Mom said.

"Oh." I had always pictured Bret chasing a ball, a red kickball for some reason. Maybe because Mom was so nutty about me not chasing a ball into the street and I had connected it in my mind to Bret?

"I told her it was time for lunch," Mom said, quieter. "She said no. She always said no to lunch. Well, to everything. And I had it in my head that we had to get lunch done, because I had things to do in the afternoon and, honestly, maybe I was a little bored, playing pretending games in the yard, and I wanted to get on with the rest of the day, so I said, 'Bret! Now! Stop fussing!' And she giggled and . . ."

Mom rubbed at her left palm with her right thumb. I reached for her hand to stop her. I'd forgotten how she used to do that, and how it made my stomach all bunchy.

"She giggled and ran away from me," Mom said. "After, I tried to tell myself we were just playing until that car . . . but no. The truth is, I was annoyed, chasing her, feeling impatient that this was my life. She was giggling, but I think also really trying to get away from me, and that's why she ran into the street."

She pulled her hand away and started rubbing the palm with her thumb again.

I swallowed hard and asked, "Is that why you never get mad at me?"

"Maybe." She sniffed in hard. "Maybe it is why."

"How do you not just cry all the time?" I asked, still not facing her.

"I did," she answered softly. "For a long time it's all I did."

"And then you, what? Got over it?"

"No," Mom said. "I'll never get over it. Daddy, either. We were wrecked for so long. We're still a bit, well, jagged."

I nodded.

"Daddy never blamed me."

"I know," I said. "He doesn't."

"I don't know if I could have been as kind to him, if it had been him in the yard that awful day."

"I bet you would have," I said. "You're the nicest person in the world."

"I'm not," she said. "I try, but I fail."

"Me too," I said.

Mom shrugged. "There's some valor in trying, I suppose."

"Hadley said I'm the thing that lifted you and Daddy out of your depression."

"You certainly helped," Mom said.

"She said it's my job to always be happy, for you."

"Oh, no," Mom said. "That's not correct. That's not your job at all. You have a job, my love, but it's not to be a . . . What did you call it? A sunshine emoji or—"

"So what is it then?" I asked, a little ashamed of how needy my voice sounded. I hunched down between my knees. Tried to sound jokey. "My job."

"Just to be you," she said.

"That's nothing." I groaned. "That's not a . . . Adults

always say that: just be yourself. As if we have any choice in the matter, and as if that's one solid thing: being yourself. Who even *is* myself? Which one? This nasty one? No, thanks, then. 'Be yourself' is stupid."

"Sorry," she said.

"Sorry. Sorry. I don't even know what I'm—"

"Gracie, I'm so sorry you've been feeling like you have to always be happy. That's really unfair."

"I didn't mean you made a rule or something," I said. "I'm not accusing you."

"No," she said. "I get it. I mean, you're right: I hate when you're sad. I want to fix it immediately. Your face was made for smiling—those dimples? What a gorgeous sunshine smile you have. When you have a flicker of sadness in your eyes, I want to take it away, wave my magic wand, say no. No being sad. No being hurt, baby of mine. No feeling confused or angry."

"Right! But—"

"But that's not fair to you. You're right. I'll try, okay? When you're angry or sad or hurt or whatever, I'll try to just sit with you through that. Instead of trying to make it go away."

"I'm not saying you can't help me," I said.

"I know. But you and I, sweetie, we're gonna have to allow ourselves to be not okay sometimes."

I shrugged. "Well, I'm basically made of Teflon, so . . ."

"No, baby, you're not," Mom said.

"Everybody says I am. Teflon Girl! It's my superpower."

"Then everybody is wrong."

"No superpowers for me?"

"Gracie, stop." She placed her warm hand on mine and sat there for a few breaths before going on. "You can feel not okay sometimes. It won't destroy you, I promise."

"Because I'm the least delicate person you ever met?"

"What?" she asked. "No."

"I just don't get it, is the thing."

"Get what?"

"Why you'd choose to love anybody. You know? What's the point? It seems like such a stupid bet, because you're practically guaranteed to end up feeling not okay. Because they might not love you back, or they'll like somebody else, or they might get over you, or they could get lost. Or die in your arms."

Mom took a deep breath.

We sat there on the stoop together, and I almost started to apologize again. But instead I took a deep breath too and looked at the scraggly flowers growing defiantly around the base of the tree in front of us, its square of dirt interrupting the sidewalk. *What's the point of you*? I wanted to ask them. *Scraggly, stupid, pointless flowers.*

"My arms can't forget how Bret felt in them," Mom whispered. "The specific weight and shape of her."

"I bet."

"But after a long time, I started to feel a little happy, before sad, thinking of her. And it hit me then how much isn't promised us."

"How much *isn't?*" I asked.

"Yes, isn't," she said. "I thought that was the deal: I'd get through the tough times with her, but I'd also be able to watch her grow up. That's all I wanted, really. But it was too much. I don't get to know grown-up Bret, and it breaks my heart every day."

"That's what I'm saying. It isn't worth—"

"But what I do get is this. This second."

"You get to sit on this dirty stoop with four bags of groceries? Wahoo."

"I get to sit here under this sky right now with you, Gracie, and hear your voice and your questions and watch you figure things out and be who you are right now with all of the complexity that entails, and I get to love you. I get to hold your beautiful, beautifully strong hand right now under that big moon hanging early and low over Downtown, and to find out that you used to think the sun rose on Madison Avenue."

"I'm some kind of genius, that's for sure."

"You are. And I get to tell you, I swear on your life, that you're not second prize to me. You never have been. You're exactly perfect, every detail of you, just as you are."

"Mom."

"Gracie, we don't get anything without also taking the risk of losing it. But here's the thing that I'm learning from you: take the risk. Barreling headlong into life, like you do? Like you've always, always done? It's the best way to find all the mind-blowing joy and silly humor the world holds. I guarantee it's still worth it."

"Doesn't seem it."

"I get to have been Bret's mom, and I get to be yours, and to be Daddy's wife, and to talk about ethics with really smart young people. I got to eat Absolute bagels with whitefish and a thick slice of tomato last Sunday, and smell the honeysuckle yesterday down by the river when so many of your sweet friends turned out to help you find Lightning. I get to sit here with you now in front of those scraggly flowers, forcing their way up into the day, against all odds there. See them?"

"Yeah," I said.

"That's it. That's all that's promised to me. Just this bit."

"And that's enough?"

"Sometimes," Mom said. "Sometimes it's not."

"Yeah," I said. "It the *sometimes it's not* that wrecks everything."

"Story of my life," Mom said.

I smiled at her.

"But that's when I take a breath and I realize that despite everything, I still have so much more in the story of my life than my heart can even hold."

I put my strong hand on her back, so our arms were braided.

She turned to me, the tears in her eyes almost overflowing. "It's so much, Gracie. It truly is."

51

WHAT?!

SIENNA: hey, so, um . . .

me: ?

SIENNA: I have to ask you something.

me: okay but listen Sienna I'm sorry. I'm sorry for everything. please can we just go back to everything is fine and we're best friends?

SIENNA: we're still best friends!

me: we are?

SIENNA: forever. I just meant I also have to, yk, talk for myself. sometimes.

me: okay. you sure did today.

SIENNA: I did, right? told Riley OFF.

me: you completely slayed her. you were awesome

SIENNA: really? it felt really good.

me: I never meant to, like, shut you down in any way . . .

SIENNA: I know. it's just sometimes easier for me to, yk, hang back and let you talk for me. which I shouldn't. but my ? is when you said you don't like Emmett . . .

me: I meant I don't LIKE HIM like him! please don't be mad at me for that you know I wasn't being mean. I love Emmett you know that!

SIENNA: are you sure?

me: about what?

SIENNA: just—any chance you maybe might LIKE HIM like him?

me: he's shorter than I am

SIENNA: sure, and he doesn't tie his shoes, but so what?

me: Sienna. I know we said we won't insult ourselves but let's be honest. I am not the LIKE-like type

SIENNA: what do you mean?

me: have you seen me?

SIENNA: uh, yes.

me: come on. my nose. my hair. my, well, everything

SIENNA: you are beautiful inside AND out, and I am obviously not the only one who knows it. ahem, somebody said something about a Rare Beauty?

me: that's a bead necklace.

SIENNA: a what? I don't think Emmett was talking about a bead necklace. do you have a concussion?

me: hahaha maybe but seriously

SIENNA: I am not even a little joking.

me: about what?

SIENNA: if Emmett asked you to go see him in the opera tomorrow night with his parents, would you say yes?

me: just me and his parents? how is that not awkward?

SIENNA: well, he'd be onstage so . . .

me: right but . . .

SIENNA: he said it wouldn't have to be like a date.

me: a date?

SIENNA: I know. unless you wanted it to be a date.

me: SHUT UP

SIENNA: well, that's the message. I'm just passing it along. it doesn't have to be a date if you don't want it to be. so—will you go? I have to text them back.

me: them? I mean sure I guess why not

SIENNA: okay, good, gtg. I'll just say unclear about if it's a date, but you'll go.

me: Sienna!!!!!!!

SIENNA: finally found something I can talk about with AJ, on the upside. . . .

me: you are the worst

SIENNA: I am the best and you love me.

me: completely true

SIENNA: you Rare Beauty, you.

me: STOP

52

IN BOCCA AL LUPO

If Bret were alive, she'd be twenty-three. She would probably have her own apartment, not live here with me and Mom and Dad. But she'd have come over today; I really think she would have—to make sure the blue dress didn't look too tight on me and to bring me something better if it did and to tell me if it looks stupid with the scarf Mom thought made it look more elegant. Bret would have brought her makeup bag and winged some liquid black eyeliner on me so I'd look just right. Mom only wears mascara and ChapStick. So that's what I mostly wear too. Bret might have more going on, makeup-wise.

She also probably would have told Mom to stop saying things like, "It's *kind of* like a first date," but complimented her on her super-quick repair of my yellow necklace.

Bret might've told us that pants would be a better idea than a dress, because the velvet on the Met's chairs kept trying to take their mini-bites out of my legs from the moment the dimming crystal chandeliers rose magically up to the high ceiling, and all through the opera, until I just tucked Mom's scarf under my thighs like a booster seat. Or maybe Bret wouldn't have been an opera fan, so she wouldn't know about the intensely scratchy seats ahead of time, and when I got home, I would tell her about that and she'd be like, *Good to know*, in case she ever got taken to the opera like me.

And then I would also tell her about sitting next to Emmett's mom for all those hours, watching Emmett in the opera *Rodelinda*. He looked like a prince up there. Well, that's what he was supposed to be: Prince Flavio. Not being weird, but just objectively, he was beautiful. And irresistible. When the bad guy threatened him with a knife, people near us gasped. When the other bad guy threatened him with a gun—for a whole song while the woman playing his mom was singing about, *Sure, go ahead, shoot my kid, you terrible!*—the whole audience was all like, *Wait, no! Don't shoot the kid!*

When he didn't, we all breathed a sigh of relief.

Emmett's shoes for the costume didn't have laces, so he didn't even have the untied thing going on. He looked very glittery up there, and so comfortable. Like he really lived there, instead of in 4C.

After the opera, we went around the side of the Met and through the stage door to wait for Emmett. It was already almost midnight, and kind of dingy where we waited, not all fancy and good-manners-designer-clothes-and-high-heels like upstairs, inside.

A bunch of other people came through the heavy slamming door before Emmett did, but eventually he showed up. His parents both gave him hugs, and his mom tried to smooth his hair down. Onstage it had been so shiny and neat, but now it was standy-uppy again, like normal. I would tell Bret, if she were alive, that the standy-uppy-ness of Emmett's hair was such a relief, because I was scared, waiting there with his parents, that I wouldn't know how to act in front of him, now that I knew he was kind of a star. But he was Emmett again, when he smiled at me with his hair all in points.

I stood to the side with his parents, outside the stage door, while he signed some fans' programs. "I don't actually have an autograph," he whispered to me as we crossed Broadway, me clomping in the black pumps. "I just write my name in script, and messy."

"Good call," I whispered back.

Even though it was after midnight, we went out to get some food at Cafe Fiorello. Emmett's mom said she'd gotten the okay from my parents ahead of time: "Don't worry." I texted them anyway. Mom texted back: **Yes! Have fun!**

We sat at a booth, me and Emmett on one side and his parents on the other. I told him, behind the tall menus, that he was really good in the opera. He thanked me for coming. We were like pretend grown-ups, though only one of us was in fancy clothes by then, with her mother's scarf stuffed into her purse, because who remembers how to put that thing back on right? The other was in his gray jeans, red hoodie, and untied sneakers.

"Sorry I'm so stinky," he said.

"It's okay," I said.

"Really?" he asked. "Because I can fully smell myself, and it's foul."

"Yeah, it's pretty intense," I admitted.

He laughed. "Told you. Wanna share profiteroles?"

"Sure," I said. I didn't know what profiteroles were or how to spell that, so I didn't even know where on the menu to look to check them out, but weirdly my hands were shaking, so I was like, whatever. It's probably not sautéed liver, which is so far the one thing I really can't manage to eat, so I just promised myself it would be fine.

"Do you mind if I go say hi to a friend?" Emmett asked us.

His parents and I didn't mind, so he got up and walked across the restaurant aisle to some huge people in a booth by themselves, eating steaks. The woman laughed the most joyous, musical laugh I've ever heard, which made me realize she was one of the main people from the opera—the one who played his aunt or something. I may have fallen a tiny bit asleep in a few places, so some of the details of the opera's plot may have been slightly unclear to me, and also, it was the middle of the night, so things were starting to take on a dreamish quality.

Emmett pointed back at us. The people eating steaks smiled and waved. They were right out of a Maurice Sendak book. We waved back. The waiter came over as Emmett was slipping back into the booth, and Emmett ordered the profiteroles for us to share and then whispered that the woman is his friend Stephanie something and the guy is her husband and they are amazing. I just listened and nodded while Emmett told us about funny conversations they've had and tricks they've played on one another backstage.

Emmett is one of my best friends, and yet he has this whole other life where he's friends with opera stars and has inside jokes with grown-ups.

I guess you really never know a person completely.

After a while the waiter brought our profiteroles—they were little puffs of cake with ice cream nestled inside, the most beautiful little lumps of ice cream sandwich spheres you can imagine. And then the waiter poured chocolate syrup on top of them from a silver lantern-thing held high above the table. It was seriously like being in a fantasy. The chocolate syrup smelled like night in winter. When we dug in with our spoons, the heat from the chocolate melted the vanilla ice cream just a bit.

I've never tasted anything so perfect.

The part I would leave out when I told Bret, if she were alive and staying over for a sleepover in my room so she could hear all about it when I got home, is the part where I fell asleep in the taxi heading home and maybe drooled a tiny bit on Emmett's father's suit jacket. But I would tell her all the rest of it, including that Emmett's parents got off on the fourth floor and told him he could ride up to the eighth with me but then to come right back down. We were quiet in the elevator the rest of the way up, and on the short walk from it to my door. He gave me a hug between Never Gonna Happen Guy's door and my door, before I unlocked it, and I didn't even mind how stinky he smelled.

That's how good the night was.

And also the hug.

53

WAIT, WHAT?

EMMETT: You still up?

me: kind of

EMMETT: Can you do me a favor?

me: sure!

EMMETT: Open your front door.

me: why?

EMMETT: You'll see.

54

NEVER GONNA HAPPEN, OR

I stepped into the cool hallway, not letting my door close behind me. Nobody was in the hall. I was in pajama bottoms and a T-shirt, no bra—hello, I was in bed, teeth brushed and trying to fall asleep already. Why would Emmett text me to open my door? I looked down at the welcome mat, thinking maybe he left me a note? Nope.

Realistically, why would he slip upstairs after we'd said good night, to leave me a note on my welcome mat? That would be amazing and, okay, romantic, but—so, right: obviously not. I was just tired. It had been a crazy long week. Being fourteen is so far way more intense than thirteen ever was.

Maybe he tucked something under the mat? I bent down

to lift it, keeping the door open with my foot. Just what I needed was to lock myself out and have to ring the doorbell to wake my parents up—or have to sleep in the hall.

Nothing under the mat but dust. As I started standing up, the door beside mine opened. Never Gonna Happen Man's door. Oh great, just who I needed to see at three in the morning.

But no. It was Emmett, in his pajama pants, a white T-shirt, and his red hoodie. Opening Never Gonna Happen Man's door.

From the inside.

He smiled.

"What are you doing in there?" I asked.

"Shhh," he said. "Can you go get Lightning?"

"Why?"

"For a race," Emmett said, and swung the door open behind him.

I looked in. There were candles lining Never Gonna Happen Man's hallway, from the entry all the way down the hall, turning it golden and flickery.

Taped onto the floor beside Emmett's sock-covered feet was a piece of construction paper, faded green with the edges almost gray, and the word *START* in Emmett's uneven handwriting in the middle. Masking tape stretched across the floor's polished wooden planks just on the other side of the sign. Way down the hall was a matching strip of masking tape and piece of construction paper, this one faded red, with *FINISH!* in Emmett's bubble letters, surrounded by illustrations of smiling hairy potatoes.

"I like the hairy potatoes," I said.

"Those are candles."

"On the finish sign."

He looked down the hall. "Where?"

"All around *FINISH!*"

"The balloons?"

"Oh," I said.

"Why would I draw hairy potatoes?" he asked.

"I don't know."

"Though, sure, what could be more exciting than hairy potatoes?"

"Exactly," I said. "At my next birthday I'm totally decorating with—"

That was when I noticed his rabbit, Fluff, curled patiently behind Emmett.

"Fluff!" I said. And then, "Wait, Emmett—did you steal the key to this apartment? Or pick the lock? We could get arrested! We're totally breaking and entering!"

"Well, not breaking," he said, flipping the secret switch on the door up and down. "Remember? So, just entering. But, Gracie?"

"What?"

"Nothing. Just. I like that you said *we* could get arrested."

"Well, sure, obviously I'd be going straight to jail with you, but wait, how did you— When did you flip the switch?"

"Shhh. Remember the other day when we were talking here and Never Gonna Happen Man came out?" he reminded me. "I flipped it while he was grabbing his stuff."

"You were planning this whole thing then?"

"I've been planning it since we were six," he said.

"Emmett!"

"Some version of it anyway. Grab Tempus. Ticktock."

"Hey."

"Yeah?"

"Nothing." I tried to pull down my smile as I dashed back into my apartment to grab Lightning from the corner of my room. I slipped my red hoodie on, on my way, to compensate for the lack-of-bra. And in solidarity with Emmett.

At the last second I grabbed my awesome hat, too, to wear for the big race.

When I got back into the other apartment, Emmett was kneeling at the start line, holding Fluff gently between his hands.

"Should I let the door close?" I asked.

"Sure."

I did, and then knelt beside him.

"Ready?" he asked.

I nodded. Not lying. "Ready."

"Set, go," he said, and we both let go of our pets.

Lightning started marching purposefully down the hall. Fluff stayed tight and huge in his soft ball of furriness.

"Ha!" I couldn't believe it. "Go, Lightning!"

"Fluff!" Emmett whispered fiercely, nudging his butt. "Go! Go! *Fugit!*"

Fluff gave him a one-eye-open look like, *Back off, buster.*

Lightning kept marching steadily away from us, clomping against the wall with her left legs most of the time, even when she had to shove candles out of her way to move forward.

"This is amazing!" I yelled. "Yes! Lightning! Did they read the fable?"

"Fluff!" Emmett urged. "We practiced! You know what to do!"

"You practiced, you cheat?"

"Fat lot of good it did me. Fluff! You're humiliating me!"

Lightning stopped just short of the finish line and turned around like, *Really? You gonna sprint up here, make it a race, dude?*

Fluff sank slowly onto his side and started snoring.

"Seriously?" Emmett asked him.

Lightning turned her head back to the project at hand and continued her trek, crossing the finish line and stepping onto the finish sign, where she finally stopped to rest on the biggest hairy potato of all.

I threw my hat into the air. "Yes!"

Emmett sat down beside his rabbit, who he scooped up into his lap. "Wow, Fluff," he whispered. "That was a pretty thorough butt-kicking we just got there, pal."

Lightning started walking again, so I ran after her. Emmett followed, Fluff cradled in his arms.

"I owe you a 16 Handles," he whispered while I picked up Lightning.

"Yes, you do," I said. "Yikes, this place is scary." There were no lights on, beyond where the candles were all lit in the hallway, and all the boxes and sheet-draped furniture or whatever was under there made the rest of the apartment look like the set of a horror movie. I stood close enough to Emmett to feel the warmth coming off him and Fluff.

"You smell like milk again," I whispered in the dark.

"I took a shower," he whispered back.

My knees got that rubber thing again. Maybe because of the darkness and unfamiliarity of the apartment we were in, it suddenly felt unclear which direction was up and, therefore, how to keep from falling.

"You okay?" he whispered.

"Yeah," I said. "Sometimes my knees . . . I think it's, like, growing pains. Or something."

"Oh, I get that," he said. "Sometimes. Too. A lot, lately."

We nodded at each other in the almost-complete darkness.

"So," he said.

"So."

"We should, probably . . ."

"Yeah."

"Do you wanna . . ."

"Wanna what?"

"Help me blow out the candles?"

"Oh," I said. "Yeah, sure."

He grabbed his red wagon from around the corner near the hallway and placed Fluff down on his favorite blanket that was waiting there in it. I put Lightning down in the hallway, facing toward the door, and went along one wall, blowing out the candles and placing them in the wagon while Emmett did the same on the other side.

"Does your mom know you took her candles and—"

"No!" He looked just behind him. "They're asleep, I hope, and I was super quiet. Is your tortoise just taking a victory lap now? That's kind of braggy, Sight Gag!"

Lightning walked over Emmett's foot, in answer.

When we each had only one candle to go, I said, "Wait—the signs." I skidded down the hall and pulled up the finish line and the sign, while Emmett did the same at the start.

"Which sign do you want to keep?" he asked. "I'll keep the other one."

"And nobody will know what they're from."

"Except Lightning and Fluff, who will never tell—right, guys?"

Fluff was snoring again, but Lightning cocked her head slightly to the side as she passed us.

"Who would even believe this craziness?" I said, imitating the Lightning voice Emmett had used when he first met her. I hoped he'd remember.

"Story of my life," he said in the same voice. So, yeah.

"You take Start," I said.

"You just want to keep the best darn hairy potatoes ever to grace a finish sign."

"I do," I said.

He opened the door and pulled the full wagon out into the public hallway.

"Should we keep it unlocked?" I asked, grabbing my awesome hat from behind the door.

"Finally have our clubhouse?" he asked.

We smiled in the bright lights. He clicked the secret switch closed.

"Once in a lifetime," I whispered.

"Yeah. Plus, you know, jail."

"Yeah. And they'd probably split us up, so . . ."

"Yeah. Let's never let that happen," he said, heading to the elevator, pulling the wagon behind him.

"Never gonna happen," I whispered, but I don't know if he heard that over the dinging of the elevator opening.

55

FIRST CHOICE

Lightning wandered around my room before finding a cozy spot by my radiator. She wedged herself in and settled down to sleep. My role model. I flopped onto my bed and wished, by habit, my sister were alive and in the room with me. But then again, maybe not. This was all mine. I hung the finish/hairy potato sign up on the wall beside my pillow and lay there, smiling like an idiot at it until my phone buzzed.

EMMETT: Quick question.

me: okay

EMMETT: What is your LEAST favorite type of date?

a. that kind that's basically a freakishly big raisin

b. a political candi-

c. one where you basically spend the whole time with the boy's parents, but, on the upside, you do get to eat half a serving of the most delicious profiteroles in Manhattan and then trounce him and his rabbit in a fable-race

d. a news up-

Before I could do more than smile, another text came through.

EMMETT: If you are considering saying c is your least favorite type of date, please remember that those big ugly raisin things are disgusting—why do they even have those?

me: oh come on it's definitely a. those things are terrifying. not just the worst type of date but the worst things ever besides maybe war and a few of the major diseases

EMMETT: Okay, cool, thanks, bye.

me: also not hugely into political candi- or news up-

EMMETT: Like, they're fine, right, but if you had to rank them . . .

me: yeah neither of those would get ranked BEST either

EMMETT: Cool, cool, same here. I mean, I actually like political candi- and news up- types of dates, but still, yeah, same. Not BEST. So . . .

me: Emmett?

EMMETT: Yeah?

me: was it always, I mean . . . were you the one who, when AJ and Sienna were texting . . .

EMMETT: Favorite types of text:

3. Con-

2. Sub-

1. Those

me: wait so

EMMETT: Hey, let's go to 16 Handles tomorrow after we sleep late. I don't want to end middle school with debts.

me: yeah sure sounds good

EMMETT: May take me a while to fall asleep.

me: same here

EMMETT: GN

me: gn

EMMETT: Stay whelmed.

me:

56

THE POSSIBILITY OF IMPOSSIBILITY

Completely overwhelmed.

Like can*not* even blink, is how much beyond whelmed I am.

Would not make travel blinking team.

Emmett.

No way.

But at the same time:

Of course.

Of course.

Turn the page for a look at

rachel vail's

next novel—

1

"EVERYBODY STAND NEXT to your best friend," the gym teacher said.

I bumped Ava's shoulder with mine.

We were already standing next to each other, of course.

We've been best friends since third grade, basically since the day she moved here. No. A few weeks after. Still, nearly forever. It's not like we were making a big, momentous decision right there in front of the entire eighth grade. Everybody knows Ava and I are best friends.

So I wasn't worried or anything. Knowing, hundred percent, that you can choose her, and that your best friend will of course choose you right back, right away, in front of everybody, no hesitation? Best feeling in the world.

But Ava didn't bump me back.

I rolled my eyes at Ava and whispered, "We're not even supposed to have best friends, I thought."

It's a rule at Snug Island Primary School: *We Are All Friends*

Here! There's a poster saying that at the entrance. Ava and I make fun of how fake it is. *Come on in and start your day with a lie, kids!* We walk under those words literally every day: *We Are All Friends Here!* The only SIPS teacher who'd ever admit it's not exactly true, that we're maybe not all friends, not all equal friends, don't even necessarily like each other all that much? It *would be* Ms. Andry, the ancient gym teacher. She's so over it, no time for that politically correct fakery. Ava and I love how fully fried Ms. Andry is.

Ava wasn't saying anything back to me.

She was looking at her sneakers.

I looked at her sneakers too.

That's why I saw her sneakers step-together-step away from me.

Toward Britney.

I smiled at Ava. My mom says, *Smiles, sunshine, and a quick cleanup make everything better!* "Why is Ms. Andry always so extra?" I whispered to Ava.

Ava always says, *Why is Ms. Andry so extra?*

This time, Ava didn't say anything.

"I mean, what's even her actual plan?" I whispered.

Ava forced out a little one-ha laugh. But she still wouldn't look at me.

Ms. Andry pointed her bony witch finger right at me. "You!" she said.

Do not pee in your pants, Niki, I told myself.

"Who are you with?" she barked at me.

I was very busy not peeing in my pants so did not have

a chance to answer evil Ms. Andry at that time.

"Who's your person?" Ms. Andry barked at Ava, having realized I was worthless.

"Britney," Ava said.

"Britney? That's somebody's *name*?" Ms. Andry asked. "Which one is Britney?"

Ava pointed her thumb at, well, Britney.

Everybody knows Britney. Britney, Isabel, and Madeleine. They're the Squad. Even Ms. Andry had to know that.

Britney leaned toward Ava, my best friend, and whispered into her ear. Ava's heart-shaped mouth puckered into a smile.

"So who's yours?" Ms. Andry asked me. Trying again.

I was watching Ava. She was whispering something back to Britney. The two of them flicked their eyes toward me. When they saw I was watching them, they turned quickly away, in unison.

"This isn't calculus, kids," Ms. Andry barked. "Just pick your best friend; I don't care who's your partner. There's an even number of you people, come on."

"What if our best friend isn't here?" Bradley asked.

"Oh, like you have a best friend," Chase said.

"Eat dirt, Chase," Bradley said. "Your best friend is your mom."

"My best friend is *your* mom!" Chase said back.

Ava and the Squad were all cracking up at the boys and their loud dissing. Bradley and Chase are best friends. They, along with Robby and Milo, are the boys who Britney, Isabel, and Madeleine hang out with. They have nothing to do with me and Ava anymore. Robby and Milo live next door to me, and we used to play together all the time, but now they glowed up and I, well, haven't.

"It doesn't matter," Ms. Andry interrupted the boys. "You two lugs can work together. Just choose a partner. Let's go. Who's left without a friend?"

I raised my hand a little, pushed it up into the air, into the concrete-air of shame weighing it down.

Across the gym, Holly Jones raised her hand too.

No. No. *You can't go backward.*

"Fine," Ms. Andry said. "You and you." She pointed at Holly Jones, and then at me. Holly walked across the gym toward me.

I kept my eyes on my feet on the high-gloss gym floor. Same sneakers as Ava's, one size bigger because my feet are disproportionately huge for my body. Same style, though: Superstars. Got them together, Ava's mom's treat. Ms. Andry was explaining the exercise we were supposed to do, something called trust falls. I didn't listen to the instructions because I couldn't hear anything but the ocean drowning me from inside my head.

Also because I didn't care.

Holly was saying something, next to me.

I don't know what, because I was very focused on not yelling, YOU ARE NOT MY BEST FRIEND. AVA IS MY BEST FRIEND. WHAT IS HAPPENING.

I gritted my teeth against it and tried to hear what Holly was saying.

"Who does she think she is, Noah?" Holly whispered out of the side of her mouth.

"What?" I managed. "Noah who?" Ugh, just what I needed was to hear about some cousin of Holly's named Noah, or some kid named Noah she knew from some retreat her weird, crunchy hippie family went on or something. *I NEED TO TALK TO AVA*, I was thinking. *I NEED TO SORT THIS OUT. I AM NOT BEST FRIENDS WITH YOU ANYMORE, HOLLY.*

"Noah! You know, Noah, loading up the ark?" Holly asked.

"I'm not religious," I said.

"Me either," Holly whispered. "As you know! But you know, like, two by two?"

"Right," I said. Right, except me. Like the unchosen llama or hippopotamus or squirrel, I was suddenly and publicly alone.

Paired with this, what, porcupine? Or, to be fair, koala. Whatever, something slightly exotic and sweet. But not two of a kind with me *at all*.

What happened to the animals stranded alone like that on the ground in front of the ark? The left-out animals, the third ones? I'd never thought about them before. Did they slink away, or did they strike?

If you're the third lion, you're dead.

Worse than dead, being the third lion, the extra elephant: condemned to the rising flood. Pre-dead, and knowing it.

Knowing, as you watch the other animals go two by two,

that there'd be no place for you inside the ark, no safety. That this is your fate, the end of the line for you. You'd just have to stand there in the drizzle. Alone, abandoned. An unchosen elephant alongside the third koala, maybe, but not half a pair, so basically alone. A random. Watching the two elephants who'd just been right beside you, one of them the one you'd expected to be your partner, as they swish their tails (ponytails) behind them in self-satisfied unison, going giggling up the gangplank onto the ark.

Feeling the floodwaters rise around your sagging ankles.

Ava was catching Britney. Britney was falling, backward, gracefully, toward Ava. *Drop her,* I wished horribly at them. My mom thinks I am nice. I am obviously not.

The two of them were laughing. Shrieking, just like Madeleine and Isabel, who were also falling backward at each other, taking turns.

I looked full-on at Holly for the first time, with her thick blue-framed glasses, her short cloud of black hair. She was looking back at me. Her face was serious, her mouth a straight line.

Worse than alone, I thought at her sweet, solemn face.

She turned around. I held out my arms for her to fall backward toward me. I felt her pouf of weight hit my arms, and stumbled to not drop her. I succeeded, but it was close.

She was light.

She stood up and faced me again without smiling. "Your turn," she said.

"No, thanks," I said.

"You can trust me," she said. Her eyes are huge and gray, like a manga drawing.

I turned my back to her.

I let myself fall, but not because I trusted Holly. How could I?

Her. Anybody.

I let myself fall backward because who even cares.

She caught me.

Whatever.

It's not like falling flat on the floor would have made my day worse.